DEBRA**WEBB**

CATHERINE**MANN**

JOANNE**ROCK**

ABOUT THE AUTHORS

Debra Webb's romantic-suspense publishing career was launched in September 2000. Since then this award-winning, bestselling author has had more than fifty novels published. Visit her on the Web at www.debrawebb.com.

RITA® Award winner **Catherine Mann** blasted onto the scene five years ago and already has over twenty books on the shelves in multiple languages. Also a Booksellers' Best winner and five-time RITA® Award finalist, she has spent the past nineteen years following her military flyboy husband around the country with their four children in tow, currently landing in the Florida panhandle. Catherine enjoys hearing from readers and chatting on her Web site message board—thanks to the wonders of wireless Internet that allows her to cyber-network with her laptop by the ocean! For more information, visit her Web site at www.catherinemann.com.

Joanne Rock's year of living in St. George, Utah, began her interest in Las Vegas, and she loved crossing miles of bare desert to arrive in this glittering oasis. The *Bet Me* anthology provided a chance to apply her memories and work with two wonderful friends. A two-time RITA® Award nominee and Golden Heart winner, Joanne is the author of thirty books ranging from medieval historicals to sexy contemporaries. A former college teacher and public relations coordinator, she has a master's degree in English from the University of Louisville and started writing when she became a stay-at-home mom. Learn more about Joanne's work at www.joannerock.com.

DEBRA**WEBB**
CATHERINE**MANN**
JOANNE**ROCK**

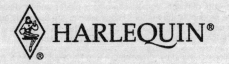

BET ME

HARLEQUIN®

TORONTO • NEW YORK • LONDON
AMSTERDAM • PARIS • SYDNEY • HAMBURG
STOCKHOLM • ATHENS • TOKYO • MILAN • MADRID
PRAGUE • WARSAW • BUDAPEST • AUCKLAND

ISBN-13: 978-0-373-83715-1
ISBN-10:   0-373-83715-1

BET ME

Copyright © 2007 by Harlequin Books S.A.

The publisher acknowledges the copyright holders of the individual works as follows:

THE ACE
Copyright © 2007 by Debra Webb

THE JOKER
Copyright © 2007 by Catherine Mann

THE WILDCARD
Copyright © 2007 by Joanne Rock

www.eHarlequin.com

Printed in U.S.A.

CONTENTS

THE ACE   9
Debra Webb

THE JOKER   115
Catherine Mann

THE WILDCARD   223
Joanne Rock

THE ACE
Debra Webb

PROLOGUE

Thursday

SEVEN A.M. WAS JUST too early for her to pay attention after a late shift on the Strip the night before. Sergeant Clarissa Rivers trudged to the coffeemaker and poured herself a second cup of coffee. She didn't know why she bothered—she winced as she took a swig—cops were the absolute worst coffee makers on the planet. The nice folks assigned to the Las Vegas Metropolitan Police Department were no different.

Clarissa resisted the urge to gag and sat her cup aside. Fifteen minutes ago it had been bearable—at this point it was just plain bitter. Better to be half asleep now than suffering with acid reflux later. She scratched her arm, then stretched to get a spot between her shoulder blades.

It had started already. That confounded itching

she experienced whenever she got close to anything even resembling a maid's uniform.

Bellying up to the counter next to Clarissa, Kim Wong reached for the coffeepot. "Don't look so happy to be here." She skimmed Clarissa from head to toe, then made one of those you-are-so-hot sounds in her throat as she filled a cup. "Kinda short, very tight. You look sharp in that outfit." Kim took a sip of coffee, grimaced, then slowly wagged her head from side to side. "Except for the color. Anything in the pink family just doesn't work for a redhead."

"Tell that to the Free Throw Casino." Clarissa shot her friend and fellow officer a look before staring down in disgust at the get-up she wore. She damned sure hadn't picked the color or the garb. A maid's uniform in a vibrant shade of rose, white apron and matching white shoes designed for comfort and outright ugliness—no way was she looking sharp.

"You could have played that part…" Kim snapped her fingers as if trying to recall. "You know in that movie with Jennifer Lopez as the hotel maid?"

"Make fun all you want," Clarissa replied, "I'll be the one laughing while you're teetering around in the royal vestments of your homeland."

"Don't remind me," Kim muttered.

Even after working with Kim for years, it was hard not to be startled by her Asian beauty. Five minutes in her presence and her spunky, kick-butt personality told anyone who might think otherwise that she was no fragile princess, even if she was about to play one. Beauty, brains and brawn, all wrapped up in one compact feminine package.

"Don't you look cute!"

Clarissa and Kim turned to greet the third member of their Metro cop girls' club, Dorian Byrne. Like Kim, Dorian hadn't been forced to don her undercover uniform just yet. Clarissa's operation started at eight sharp this morning. She could hardly wait.

"Hey, Dorian." Clarissa couldn't hold back a smirk at the idea of what was to come for her other good friend. "The whole department's been dying to get a load of those long legs for ages." Dorian had some Latino heritage somewhere in her background. Just enough to give her a perpetual tan and a slightly exotic look. Short, sexy black hair. The perfect body. Another gorgeous female member of LVMPD.

Dorian threw her hands up Stop-sign fashion. "If I hear one more word about the hooker assignment," she warned, "both of you will regret it."

Kim and Clarissa exchanged a look. Dorian got the best assignment of all, in Clarissa's opinion. Going after the really bad guys in a disappearing-prostitute case. Kim's op involved stolen diamonds and Clarissa's was illegal gambling. All three included a level of personal risk and came with a short fuse—they had to get it done within seventy-two hours. But Dorian's was by far the grittiest. In any case, this was going to be one interesting weekend.

"At least," Clarissa said as she planted her hands firmly on her starched-cotton-clad hips, "you don't have to be a servant. Do you have any idea the grief I'll be taking from rich guests for the next three days?" Clarissa knew all too well from personal experience.

"Stow it, ladies," a firm male voice bellowed before Dorian or Kim could argue Clarissa's point. "We have a briefing to attend to."

Captain Bill Pearson. The boss. An attractive man in his forties, under far more stress than was healthy even for a man so fit, ambled up to the coffeepot next. The mayor, along with every other bigwig in Las Vegas, was up in arms about the rising crime rate and how tourism had been adversely affected. With the final big weekend of the summer coming up, Labor Day, in just eight days,

Operation: Clean Sweep had been set in motion. Every cop in the department had his or her segment of the Strip to spiff up. For Clarissa it was the Free Throw Casino. Kim and Dorian had casinos of their own to target. All forms, big and small, of criminal activity in the city were in for a major wake-up call during the next three days.

Pearson filled his cup and looked from one to the other. "Let's stop complaining and get to it."

"Yes, sir," Clarissa said with a snappy salute. Kim and Dorian echoed the same.

Pearson flashed an annoyed face, then headed for the briefing room.

All kidding aside, Clarissa was really worried about him. His wife of twenty years was on the verge of sending him packing if he didn't slow down on those ninety-hour workweeks.

"You know," Kim said, hesitating instead of falling in behind their fearless leader, "we should lay down a little wager to make this weekend more interesting."

Clarissa's full attention jumped back to her pals. "What kind of wager?"

Kim shrugged. "I don't know. Maybe see who gets their baddie first."

"And," Dorian added, "who gets the report filed *first*."

Kim groaned. "I hate those things."

Every cop did…except Dorian. She was a hurricane on the keyboard. Whipping out a masterful final report was like taking a breath for her. Not only was she fast on the keys, she could sum up a case in the least possible number of words.

But she had to get her perp first to win. No perp, no final report.

"I'm in," Clarissa said, never one to back down from a challenge. "What's the prize? Can't have a wager without one."

Kim and Dorian seemed to consider the possibilities.

"How about Labor Day weekend at a luxury spa?" Dorian suggested. "All expenses paid by the two losers?" She looked from Clarissa to Kim as if their fates had already been decided.

"That's a decent start, but we need more," Kim said, raising the stakes. "Something to make the extra effort really worthwhile."

"The whole week off," Clarissa suggested, "starting Monday. In addition to the spa weekend."

The three mentally tallied the cost and the number of vacation days the losing parties would each need to throw in to cover the time off.

"It's a bet," Dorian tossed out first.

Clarissa looked to Kim. This was her idea—she surely wouldn't back out now.

"I'm in," the Asian-princess-to-be confirmed.

"Then we have a bet," Clarissa said.

After they had shaken hands to seal the wager, they followed the other cops, some, like Clarissa, already dressed in costume, into the briefing room.

This was one bet Clarissa fully intended to win.

"Spa weekend," she murmured, "here I come."

CHAPTER ONE

Free Throw Casino Hotel
Room 2119

"SLOB," CLARISSA MUTTERED as she picked up the jeans from the floor. *Versace*. She shook her head. Didn't this guy have better things to do with his money? Give her Levi's any day of the week.

She had cleaned the bathroom already. Made the bed and dusted the elegant mahogany furnishings. But she couldn't vacuum without running the risk of sucking up something that cost more than a month's salary. This Mr. Jennings was a total slob. Clothes, all male, were scattered around as if he'd been in a mad frenzy to peel them off. Jeans, faded and well worn despite their designer label, plain white cotton tee and a navy silk jacket that seemed mismatched with the rest. Oh, and let's not forget the handmade Italian leather loafers.

Clarissa forced herself to neatly fold the articles of clothing and place them on the ornate credenza that served as a dresser. Some renegade brain cell made her go momentarily stupid and she sniffed the T-shirt. An earthy male scent all but overwhelmed by cheap women's perfume and not-so-cheap champagne. Clarissa was surprised she hadn't found female clothing tangled in the sheets. Clearly this guy had had company last night. She tucked the overpriced shoes next to the closet door, and then dusted her hands in finality.

All she had to do was vacuum and she was out of here.

Hopefully by now—she glanced at her wristwatch—some of the high rollers on her watch list would be up and around. So far, all three of her most likely suspects had been piled up in bed with the do-not-disturb signs out—even at 10:00 a.m.

She scratched her side through the stiff uniform. God, she was going to be covered in hives before lunch at this rate. Calamine lotion loomed in her future.

After plugging in the vacuum, she switched it on and got down to business. It was hard to believe half the morning was gone already and she hadn't even gotten close to the first suspect on her list.

Sergio Fuentes, Bogotá, Colombia.

Mark Weldon, Houston, Texas.

Rita Russo, Miami, Florida.

Those were the three VIPs that had tripped LVMPD's radar upon arrival in Sin City. All were suspected of illegal activities in their home territories. Then, of course, there was Shannon Bainbridge, the woman in charge of high-rollers gambling at the Free Throw. Clarissa suspected that Bainbridge coordinated everything on this end, but that was only a suspicion. She needed evidence.

Floors twenty-one through twenty-six were the ones of interest to Clarissa. Twenty-one through twenty-four were VIP guest suites, like this one. Twenty-five was dedicated solely to VIP gambling, with only four suites reserved for the crème de la crème of guests. The penthouse and a couple of select, private playing rooms were on twenty-six.

Fuentes, Weldon and Russo were all playing on twenty-five and twenty-six. Playing on twenty-five was a perk of being a guest on the upper floors. Getting to twenty-six required a personal invitation by a member from one of the few tables in those private rooms.

Clarissa didn't see that happening for her, but she would get as close as possible. She wasn't allowed to enter the penthouse floor without invitation and a scheduled time, not even to make the bed. Basically all she had to do was prove Bainbridge was involved and Clarissa felt confident the woman would spill her guts. Clarissa could type up her final report and win this bet. She would be seriously ready for some R & R after wearing this damned uniform for seventy-two hours.

Between the itching and the less-than-comfortable thigh holster this assignment was not going to be a pleasant one. Not to mention she had little use for the high-roller types. She'd had far too much firsthand experience with the absurdly wealthy growing up.

Clarissa shook off the thought before it could take root and spoil her day.

Goose bumps suddenly rushed over her skin and the hair on the back of her neck stood on end.

She wasn't alone.

The instinct kicked her in the gut a split second before she whirled around to come face-to-face with six feet of hard, sweaty male.

For three seconds that lapsed into ten she couldn't decide what to say. *Hello. Who the hell are you?*

Never in her life had she found herself at a total loss for words the way she was at that exact moment.

He said something but it didn't penetrate the haze of confusion or whatever the hell had just wrapped around her brain.

She blinked. "What?"

He reached around her and shut off the vacuum.

"I said—" he cleared his throat and lowered his voice "—sorry to interrupt." He plowed his fingers through his tousled blond hair. "I'm Luke Jennings. I'll try not to get in your way." He plucked at the damp shirt clinging to his chest. "But I need a shower."

Jennings. The guest assigned to this room.

"Oh." She snapped out of the ridiculous daze. What the hell just happened to her? "No problem. I'm almost finished."

"Take your time." He flashed her a quick smile then sauntered a little one-sidedly toward the en suite bath, peeling off the wet-with-sweat tank top as he went.

An expanse of nicely tanned skin drew her attention to broad, broad shoulders that tapered into a lean, narrow waist and hips...and long, muscled—really muscled—legs. She noted the slightest limp as he disappeared into the luxurious bathroom.

Jennings. Luke Jennings. Why did that name, coupled with the handsome face, seem vaguely familiar?

A memory bobbed to the surface. "Damn." Luke Jennings. The *Ace*. Professional cyclist who'd won the Tour de France five years in a row. Would have won six if he hadn't taken a nasty spill that wrecked his right knee.

That explained the limp.

Clarissa glanced at the clothes she had gathered off the floor. Oh, yeah, he would have had company last night. That was the thing with celebrity athletes. There was always a flock of women following them wherever they went. She shook her head. Didn't see the attraction. Why would any woman in her right mind chase after such a massive ego?

Just then she caught a glimpse of Jennings's naked backside as he stepped into the shower. He hadn't closed the door…but then, maybe he hadn't expected her to stare after him.

Talk about a great ass. Her mouth gaped.

Wow.

She pivoted and grabbed the vacuum's handle. Focus, Rivers. This was no time to get caught checking out some guy's buns.

Especially not this guy's.

She had an assignment and Luke Jennings was not a part of it. Nor was his amazing bod. Clarissa knew his type. Lots of money, women at every turn. Definitely not what she was looking for in her future. She'd had a guy very much like him around for as long as she could remember.

Her father had been a wealthy, handsome playboy. Not on purpose, though—she had to give him credit where credit was due. Her mother had passed away when Clarissa was only two. For years her father had played the part of widower and single father with no social life. Then the string of girlfriends and wives had begun. Every new girlfriend or wife doted on Clarissa to no end—all the way up to the part where the I-do's were exchanged. Then the new wife wanted the daughter shipped off to boarding school.

Living in so many different cities and with no fewer than a half-dozen boarding schools under her belt, Clarissa couldn't really say where home was. To some extent home had always been a fancy hotel suite with a maid seeing after her more often than not. With all the business trips and minivacations to Vegas with her father, this place ended up feeling more like home than any other city. So Clarissa had landed here in the end.

Though she felt confident she had turned out okay, her location-hopping past was no kind of life for a kid. If—major if—she ever had kids of her own, they would not be dragged around like that.

Maybe that was why she'd hit thirty recently and hadn't felt the first biological prompt for marriage, much less children. Clarissa liked her life just as it was.

Her father had set up a huge trust fund for her, but she would rather earn her own way. He couldn't understand why she would play the role of cop when she never had to worry about supporting herself.

The answer to that question wasn't so simple. Even if she could spell it out she doubted he would understand. This was something she had to do.

Taking on the bad guys, making the world a safer place. That was important to her. There definitely wasn't room for guys like Luke Jennings in her plans.

Nope. Unless he turned out to be a suspect in her op, he was off-limits.

LUKE BRACED HIS HANDS against the sleek marble of the shower walls and closed his eyes to wait out the pain. His knee throbbed like a son of a bitch. He shouldn't have run that last mile. Stupid. Really stupid.

His cycling career was over. Why the hell did he continue to fight the inevitable? Putting unnecessary stress on his knee was only going to cause him trouble in the long run. The *Ace* was gone for good.

But he couldn't just go quietly into retirement the way his agent wanted. That wasn't who Luke was.

Hell, truth was, he didn't even know himself anymore.

He braced his forehead against the cool stone. Without his career, he was just another has-been. According to his agent the best he could hope for was a couple of major product endorsements before the world found out he wouldn't be taking on another race.

So here he was in Vegas, playing celebrity emcee representing a Fortune 500 sports equipment company at a cheerleader convention. No offense to cheerleaders, but this was not what he wanted to be doing with his life.

And if the looming monumental step down in his career wasn't bad enough, all those women hung on him as if he were the only man in the city.

Luke loved women, he really did. All that female attention had been great at first. Really great. But after the first couple of years it had become less than fulfilling. These days it just made him feel empty.

Forcing himself to go through the motions of

actually showering, he scrubbed his hair and then his skin. It would be nice if washing away his disappointment were so easy. He would be lying if he said he didn't care about his inability to compete the way he used to. It would take time to get used to the idea of not being Luke Jennings, champion cyclist.

Funny thing was, the part that bothered him the most, now that he had time to think about it, was the idea of being thirty-two and unconnected. No significant other. Nothing.

As crazy as it sounded, he wanted a *real* relationship.

He shook the water from his face. "Damned crazy," he muttered.

Guys like him weren't supposed to want relationships. Staying single kept his celebrity status higher profile. Women wanted to believe he was available, and his agent had always insisted that Luke keep any long-term—meaning more than a weekend—relationship under wraps.

Luke had tried that—once. The woman had ended up walking away and selling her story to some gossip rag. He'd ended up looking like a jerk.

He stepped out of the shower and grabbed a towel and started to dry himself off. What was wrong with a guy like him wanting the real thing? An actual relationship based on mutual interest and respect? Why did everything have to be about his celebrity status and the public's perception?

Setting all that aside, how the hell was he supposed to build a relationship when he couldn't get anyone to look past the fact that he was champion cyclist Luke Jennings?

There it was. His life. The good, the bad—he glanced down at his damaged knee—and the ugly.

The soft roar of the vacuum reminded him that the maid was still in the room. He wrapped the towel around his waist and walked to the open doorway. He'd been so frustrated with his aching knee when he'd come in that he had forgotten to close the door. She probably thought he was an exhibitionist in addition to being a slob.

His gaze fixed on the lady's curvy bottom and toned legs as she went about vacuuming the thick white carpet. Leaning against the door frame, his lips tipped into a smile when she kicked aside one of his socks. She muttered something, something negative about him, judging by the irritation behind the move. He should have picked up after himself last night but he'd been too pissed off. He'd been groped by dozens of women and one had spilled a glass of champagne on him.

Somehow he'd managed to hold on to his temper while he'd excused himself. He'd had to shed no fewer than four clinging blondes en route to his room. The product sponsors had still been at the party so he'd had no choice but to quickly change and go back down.

He'd hated every minute of it. What had once felt like beefing up the value of his stock now felt like selling himself out to the highest bidder.

Sour grapes, his agent would say. He felt bitter at the idea that he couldn't race anymore and he was taking it out on the other aspects of his profession.

Maybe that was true.

The one thing he knew with complete certainty was that he could not, *could not,* get through the weekend without figuring out a way to keep the women at bay.

He scrubbed a hand over his face. Did he really just think that?

He was officially losing it. What man in his right mind didn't want women hanging on to his every word?

One who wanted a real relationship, he reminded himself.

The maid turned off the vacuum and sighed with satisfaction.

He opened his mouth to say hello at the same instant she swiveled around to survey her handiwork. Her gaze bumped into his and she made the cutest sound—not quite a squeal but far more than a gasp.

His smile widened to a grin. "Sorry. I was just about to apologize for leaving such a mess this morning."

The irritated expression she wore signaled that she wasn't buying his sincerity.

"Some…" He folded his arms over his chest and tried to decide how to explain. "Someone poured champagne all over me and I—"

She held up her hands. "That's okay, sir. You don't have to explain. Cleaning up is my job." Her eyes widened and she abruptly scratched at her side. When she realized she'd done so in front of him her face pinked.

The red hair and green eyes were gorgeous, even in the rosy-colored uniform. But it was the fullness of her lips that really made him want to know her better. There was a stubbornness about that mouth…a determination that told him she was no pushover.

The plan came in one abrupt rush.

No, he argued with himself.

His gaze locked with hers.

Maybe.

"It could work," he mumbled.

"Excuse me?" Her eyes slitted with suspicion.

Luke cleared his throat and straightened away from the door. Yes, it could definitely work. "What's your name?"

"Cris."

She said her name so hesitantly he wondered if she was afraid of him or simply worried about the rules that didn't allow her to fraternize with the guests.

"Cris," he repeated, thinking the name didn't really fit, but liking the way she looked at him when he said it. "I have a proposition for you."

The reluctance turned to outright wariness. "What kind of proposition?"

He took two steps in her direction. "One I think you'll like a lot."

CHAPTER TWO

CLARISSA HAD TO ADMIT she'd considered all the risks involved with this operation and not one of them had included being propositioned by a nearly naked man. That was the sort of hazard Dorian would be up against in her role as a make-believe hooker.

"This isn't what it sounds like," Jennings hastened to add.

She wasn't so sure about that but she let him keep talking.

"You see, I'm here helping out one of my sponsors with a cheerleading convention." He shrugged those mile-wide shoulders. "It's a sports equipment sponsor. You know how it is. You do what you have to in order to keep everybody happy, and your contract gets renewed."

She nodded, mostly because he was actually blushing behind that great tan. Watching him squirm was kind of fun. She would bet he didn't do that often. Plus, she got to admire that great bod with its golden beach-bum glow. It just wasn't fair. Her fair skin prevented her from doing anything but burning.

"Anyway, the women are…" He exhaled a mighty breath. "The women are driving me crazy. I need a break."

If he hadn't looked so genuinely at the end of his rope, she might have laughed, but this guy was honestly disgusted about the whole idea. Strange.

"People come to Vegas all the time," he began again, "and get married, then divorced when the weekend is over."

She nodded. That was true. Some did it without remembering, and then legal trouble followed. She'd had to break up a fight or two over drunken nuptials.

"Anyway, I was thinking that if you pretended to be my wife, I could keep the…er…ladies off my back and actually get through this weekend."

Clarissa did a double take. "What exactly are you asking me to do?" Now, this was bizarre. If there was a hidden camera in this room…she was going to kill the guys at the station for setting her up.

Surely Luke Jennings wasn't asking her to actually marry him and then get divorced on Monday.

"Just pretend to be my wife," he said adamantly, his hands open, palms up in a beseeching gesture. "No strings attached. Just hang on my arm and pretend to be enamored with me and I'll pay you...a year's salary...or whatever you feel is appropriate."

Did she look that desperate to him? Just when she'd decided to ask as much, she realized that he was the one who was desperate. Those big puppy-dog brown eyes were begging for her help.

Where was the famous unbeatable athlete who never gave up? The mammoth ego?

"I'm sorry, Mr. Jennings." Not only could she not do this on a wholly ethical level personally, but professionally she was here undercover. She had a job to do. And he was not on her list of potential suspects, which meant he wasn't part of her assignment. Any risks she took with her cover would be to nail a suspect. "But I would get fired if—"

"I'll take care of everything," he urged. "I know the VIP manager. I can fix it with her. You have my word."

Clarissa stood very still, absorbed those words a little more fully. It couldn't be this easy. "You know Ms. Bainbridge?" Clarissa didn't believe in coincidences, and this would definitely be one hell of a lucky coincidence. Knowing the VIP manager meant ready access to the VIP gambling rooms. At least the ones on the twenty-fifth floor.

"We both went to the University of Colorado. She graduated a couple of years before me. But, yes, I know her. She gives me a VIP suite anytime I come to town. Goes the extra mile to make my stay enjoyable."

A plan formed in Clarissa's head faster than her good friend Dorian could have typed it. "So we don't have to do anything on paper. Just pretend."

"Just pretend," he agreed.

"I'll do it," Clarissa declared, "on one condition."

He set his hands on his hips just above that precariously slung towel. "Name it."

"You get me into the high-roller games on the twenty-fifth floor and I'll gladly play the part of your wife."

He thrust out his hand without hesitation. "Done."

CHAPTER THREE

9:00 p.m.

SHE HAD MADE IT THROUGH her first afternoon as Mrs. Luke Jennings. Now it was time for him to fulfill his side of the bargain and escort her to the exclusive gaming rooms.

The paparazzi hadn't been so bad. Clarissa had gotten authorization from Pearson to deviate from protocol, and Luke had made a short announcement to the press. Easy as one, two, three.

Clarissa was now, as far as those who followed the cheesier news knew, Mrs. Luke Jennings.

Two hours in the convention center grand ballroom playing her part and she understood exactly why the man wanted a make-believe wife.

His female fans treated him like a side of beef.

Clarissa had seen men treat women that way plenty of times, but she hadn't seen women act this way since the last time she'd had to break up a fight at a Chippendales performance.

She almost felt sorry for the guy.

Almost.

The ego was there, just not nearly as prominent as she had expected.

He actually seemed like a nice guy…so far.

Her arm wrapped around his, he escorted her off the elevator and onto the twenty-fifth floor.

She leaned closer. "Thanks." His proposition had gotten her onto this floor a whole lot faster than she could have hoped for.

He glanced down at her. "Hey, after what you went through with the paparazzi and the ladies at the convention center, this is the least I can do."

Clarissa didn't bother telling him she'd lived with the paparazzi growing up. Her father hadn't been a celebrity exactly, but he'd been a very rich man and that alone had garnered him far more attention than the average Joe.

Her, too. But she'd finally managed to escape it. No one ever connected Sergeant Clarissa Rivers to child heiress Crissy Rivers. With her father's retirement to a private island, the Rivers name had followed the same route.

Thank God.

"Welcome, Mr. Jennings," a deep voice boomed

as Clarissa and Luke entered the plush private players lounge on the twenty-fifth floor.

Luke nodded to the man in the black suit who dressed exactly like a member of the president's personal Secret Service detail. House security. The folks on this level were the richest of the rich. Top-notch security and ultimate service were part of what kept clients coming back to the Free Throw over the rest of the competition.

"This is my wife," Luke said to the man, then smiled at her. "Crissy Jennings."

She kept her smile tacked in place in spite of his using the pet name she disliked. Her father had called her that growing up. But, then, he was her father and so she had cut him a break. No one else had ever dared call her by that nickname.

"Mrs. Jennings," the gentleman, evidently the chief of security, said as he executed a slight bow. "My name is Douglas. Anything you need you let me know."

"Thank you, Douglas." She inclined her head in acknowledgment of his offer.

So this was the life her father had enjoyed when he'd brought her to Vegas all those times. She had always spent her nights in the room with a nanny or maid. She'd never been allowed to venture into this territory even after she'd reached the necessary age. For the most part, her father had been extremely protective.

Luke led her deeper into the room where poker games were in progress and roulette tables were spinning like colorful tops. Craps, slots, it was all there. Cigar and cigarette smoke hung in the air, making her lungs seize. Plasma televisions were suspended on every wall, showing major sporting events from all around the world for the viewing pleasure of those present.

"What's your pleasure, my lady?" Luke offered. "Poker?" He grinned. "Roulette?" He gestured to the tables on the balcony beyond the windows overlooking the infamous Strip. "Or would you prefer a drink and quiet conversation?"

Clarissa disentangled herself from her escort. "I think I'd like to mingle alone for a while. Do you mind?"

He didn't have to worry about any cheerleaders showing up here, so she wouldn't need to provide that barrier for now. Surely he could entertain himself for a couple of hours.

"I'll be at the bar."

As he walked away, she couldn't help feeling he was disappointed somehow.

He would just have to get over it. She had a job to do and they had a deal.

Clarissa took a deep breath and surveyed the room once more. Lots of plush red carpet and gold embellishments. This was where she would find her targets.

Time to go to work.

She'd soaked her torso down in calamine lotion and let it dry before slipping into the gorgeous dress Jennings had had delivered to her newly assigned room right next to his. As hard as she'd tried, he had refused to take the dress back. She'd gone home for some things of her own since her strategy had changed and she would be staying at the hotel. Shannon Bainbridge had authorized Clarissa's release from duties for this favor to Jennings. Clarissa studied the gorgeous dress he'd bought for her. She hadn't owned anything like this since she had turned twenty-one and was introduced to society at her debutante ball. Gold sequins. Strapless. Form-fitting. Matching stilettos. She looked damned good for a cop.

It would be hell getting to her .22 since it was strapped to her thigh and her dress hit the floor, but she wasn't anticipating needing it here. She felt certain that if she went for it, Douglas would take her out in one shot. Security at this level was highly trained and intensely focused. The badge

stuffed into her tiny purse might not be as persua-
sive here as other places.

She spotted Sergio Fuentes first. His devilishly
dark good looks made her think of steamy
jungles. If, as was suspected, he was here to buy
into the illegal activities, then he would be
making contact with Bainbridge—if she was the
one heading this operation.

That was the thing. In Vegas the motto was
"pretty much anything goes" when it came to
gambling—as long as it was on the up-and-up and
was played by the rules. But the intelligence they
had gathered indicated that this was a different
kind of gambling. The behind-the-scenes kind that
filled the pockets of organized crime, from gun
runners to drug distributors.

If Clarissa could find solid evidence that Bainbridge was up to something, LVMPD would clean
house with the casino owner's blessing. Any
money that was going to other interests was not
finding its way to the owner's bank account. Then,
of course, there were the city's and state's interests that would be overlooked, as well.

Fuentes had taken a seat at the bar, ordered a
drink and lit his cigar. Clarissa wandered in that
direction, thankful that Jennings was chatting with
another man at the other end.

Clarissa leaned against the bar next to where Fuentes had perched on a stool. "White wine," she told the bartender.

In the mirror behind the bar she watched Fuentes watching her while she waited for the wine. He had the typical South American male reputation for womanizing.

"Surely the lady is not drinking alone," he said when he'd looked his fill.

The bartender sat the stemmed glass in front of her and she took a refreshing sip before answering the question or even meeting Fuentes's gaze.

Clarissa scooted onto the stool next to him. "I'm not now." She peered up at him from beneath her lashes as she took another tiny sip.

He smiled, showed off a mouthful of movie-star quality teeth. "I have not seen you here before, *señora.*"

She thrust out her hand. "I'm Cris Jennings."

Fuentes took her hand but instead of shaking it, he brushed his lips across the back of it. "I am honored to make your acquaintance, Cris Jennings."

She had to give the man credit. The way he said her name was very sexy. But she could have done without his smearing his DNA on her skin.

"And you are?" she inquired as she pulled her hand away.

"Sergio Fuentes." He took a long drag from his cigar before allowing his gaze to blatantly rove her body. "So, you like?" He gestured to the room at large as he exhaled a blue plume of smoke.

Clarissa glanced around the room with utter indifference. "It's actually rather boring." She sipped her wine, then licked the rim of the glass to catch a drop before it slid downward. "I only came because my husband made me." She sent a pointed look at Luke Jennings. "And then he ignores me."

Fuentes studied Jennings a moment. "That is a shame, *señora*. Your husband is not so smart."

She slid off the stool. "Well, Mr. Fuentes, it was very nice to meet you." She sent him another smile as she walked away. She felt his eyes on her all the way across the room. At least she'd gotten his attention.

Rita Russo entered the room, an escort on either side of her, and jewels dripping from every possible surface. Clarissa's attention shifted to her. If Weldon showed up, all suspects would be accounted for and all she would have to do was get as close as possible to each one.

"Hey."

Startled, Clarissa looked up to find her pretend husband loitering next to her. She pushed a smile into place. "Hey, yourself."

"You like the feel of power up here?" he asked, his curiosity settling on the latest arrival. "Lots of money to throw around."

"You're not a gambling man, Mr. Jennings?"

He shook his head. "Nope. I'd rather donate it to a good cause than do this."

Was he trying to impress her? She had to admit that would certainly do the trick but she would have to see the proof to believe it. Growing up around people exactly like him, with great financial means and extensive power, had made her a little skeptical. She and her father still didn't see eye to eye on the fairness of extreme wealth. That she donated large portions of her annual trust installment remained a sore spot between them.

Mark Weldon entered the room then, and Clarissa's full attention returned to her assignment. She left Jennings with his Scotch and her assurance that she would talk to him later as she moved into action. Working the room had to be the only item on her agenda just now. Clarissa hadn't done this in a long time, but she had learned how to make a crowd her own from the best privileged socialites on the manhunt circuit.

She just hadn't turned it on in a few years.

LUKE HAD TO SAY, in all his years of doing big social to-dos and fund-raisers, he'd never watched anyone better at wooing a crowd. His pretend wife owned the room. The woman should be doing this for a living. He would never have expected someone in the housekeeping side of the gambling business to be able to handle a situation like this quite so well.

It was only midnight and already everyone knew her name and wanted her at their table. Luke hung at the bar and just enjoyed the show. Strangely enough, it didn't bother him at all that the lady preferred rubbing shoulders with the high rollers to spending time with him. He found it oddly refreshing.

This was what the lady had asked for in return for playing the part of his wife for the weekend. The least he could do was stay out of her way.

But there was this one guy. One of those Antonio Banderas look-alikes. Now that dude bugged him. He seemed to appear at Cris's side out of nowhere. Whispering in her ear. Smiling. Offering her a fresh drink.

Luke didn't like the guy at all.

In fact, he was sick of him.

Before good sense could kick in, Luke strode across the room to join the woman who was supposed to be his new bride. He snaked his arm around her waist and pulled her against him, then leaned down and whispered, "Baby, don't you think it's time we called it a night? After all it is our honeymoon." He put his lips right against her ear to say the rest. "We don't want anyone getting suspicious."

She shivered. Whether the sensation had been a pleasant experience or motivated by irritation at his forwardness he couldn't say, particularly since she avoided looking at him.

"But I was just beginning to have fun, honey-pie," she murmured back. The look in her eyes as she met his was unmistakable. *Back off.*

A deal was a deal. He took a step away. Tried not to show his impatience and irrational annoyance. They weren't actually married. They didn't even know each other. She could talk to anyone she pleased. There was no need for her to be in a hurry to go anywhere with him.

Fuentes appeared again, setting Luke's teeth on edge.

He passed a card to Cris. "Join me tomorrow night at Club Red on the twenty-sixth floor. I would very much like the pleasure of showing you that world." He glanced at Luke. "Bring your husband if you wish." Fuentes swaggered away with all the confidence of a man who had just trumped all the offers in the room.

Unreasonably, outrage roared through Luke.

"We can go now," his make-believe wife said.

His gaze collided with hers. "We can go?" he parroted like a total idiot.

She nodded, tucked the card Fuentes had given her into her sequined clutch purse. "Yes. I'm finished for tonight."

And just like that the lady took Luke by the arm and led him from the room.

He wasn't sure how it had happened. But somehow, she was in charge. Maybe she had been all along.

He'd thought he was…but he'd been wrong.

CHAPTER FOUR

Friday, 1:00 p.m.

CLARISSA WORKED HARD at not dozing off as the luncheon speaker droned on about the high-quality helmets and other safety equipment his company manufactured.

Luke Jennings had been named top athlete for the third year running by the company. She'd heard the *Ace* this and the *Ace* that at every turn. Funny thing was, Luke seemed to flinch every time that name was tossed out.

She remembered to applaud at all the right times but otherwise her mind was zoned out. She needed sleep. Last night had been a late one. Luke had knocked on the connecting door between their suites and proceeded to talk her ear off for the next two hours. She couldn't decide if he was just lonely or if he was curious. Not that he asked her many questions, but the few he did had been loaded with interest.

Maybe the guy was simply unaccustomed to carrying on a conversation with a woman who wasn't poised to jump his bones, and he enjoyed the novelty. Not that she would mind jumping his bones, but this was work. She could not let any aspect of this little you-scratch-my-back-I'll-scratch-yours endeavor get personal.

And he had to stop buying her gifts. She had been awakened this morning by yet another delivery. More expensive clothing, two formal gowns, three cocktail dresses. All with matching accessories. He'd insisted that it was nothing more than what she would need to get through the weekend.

Oh, and she mustn't forget the flowers. The room was brimming with roses in every imaginable color.

Pictures of the two of them had made a few of the gossip rags. So far no connection between her and her past had been mentioned. But it was only a matter of time. Hopefully this weekend would be over before that happened.

Her caution radar went on alert as he leaned nearer to whisper something in her ear. She wished he wouldn't do that. No matter how hard she tried she always ended up shivering like a damned hormone-driven teenager whenever he got that close. How the hell could this be happening to her? She never got all giddy and gooey over some guy. And that was exactly how she felt.

How was she supposed to win this bet if she kept going stupid?

"I am so bored," he murmured.

She had to smile. For a guy who had gotten rich on endorsements he didn't appear to have a lot of patience where these functions were concerned.

Turning her face to his ear, she whispered, "One more hour and you'll be free." He smiled, causing her lips to brush his jaw.

There was no way to miss the tiny hitch in his respiration.

Was it possible that she could do to him what he so easily did to her? She avoided thinking the specifics since each and every one was so, so off-limits. Why couldn't she have had a reaction like this any other time? To someone who wasn't such a dangerous combination? Celebrity and professional athlete were two major no-no's in her book. A formula for trouble.

His lips teased her ear again. "We should think of something fun to do."

Several explicit possibilities came instantly to mind.

Going down this road is a big mistake, Clarissa.

But, hey, she was only human and this guy was hot.

The crowd burst into an enthusiastic standing ovation at whatever the speaker said last. She and Luke managed to get to their feet and do the same despite the glaring distraction that had clearly affected them both.

For the next half hour Luke was inundated with handshakes and praise. Everyone appeared to love him, but she wondered how much of that was hype—the expected responses. It would be difficult to balance friends in his world. She remembered those trials all too well. Who did you trust? Who did you allow into the inner sanctum of your private world? Did he or she like you for you or for your money?

Questions she was ever so thankful she didn't have to worry about answering anymore.

That was the thing. Being with a guy like Luke for real came with far too many complications. With a few inches' distance between them now, her good sense kicked back into gear. She couldn't do that.

No way. No how.

LUKE PULLED HIS TIE LOOSE as he lowered into a chair in his suite. Finally. He massaged his throbbing knee and grimaced. A pain pill would help about now but he just couldn't go there unless it was an absolute last resort. He needed to stay fully in control of all his faculties this weekend.

On the bedside table the telephone's flashing red light indicated that he had received a voice mail. Odd. His manager surely would have called his cell phone. Could be someone on the sponsor's team, he supposed.

With a grunt he levered himself to his feet and limped to the bedside table. If the call was from another cheerleader who wanted him to join their squad for dinner he was going to scream. As much as he loved short skirts and toned thighs...he was just tired.

He punched the necessary buttons to retrieve the call.

Cris, this is Sergio. I was hoping we could have a drink this afternoon. My room is 2514. I will be expecting your call.

Sergio?

The ambitious Latin guy from last night.

More of that uncalled-for irritation filtered through Luke. It wasn't like he had any claim on Cris but for all *Sergio* knew she was Luke's wife. What kind of man went around hitting on another man's wife?

Luke dropped the receiver back into its cradle and glanced at the connecting door. He should tell her. The message was for her, after all. Maybe this Sergio had something to offer. It wouldn't be fair for him to deny her the opportunity to snag a rich guy. Who knew? Maybe that was why she had taken a job as a hotel maid in a casino in the first place.

Luke exhaled a disgusted breath and strode to the connecting door. He winced with every step. *Damn it.*

He rapped on the door and waited.

When it opened he was surprised to find her dressed in sleek black slacks and a white peasant-style blouse, looking as if he'd just caught her on her way out.

"Yes?" She slipped the final button of her blouse into its closure.

He hitched his thumb toward the phone. "You had a message from Sergio." Keeping the disapproval out of his tone was impossible. "He wants to have a drink with you this afternoon. Room 2514."

Cris searched his face. "Do we have plans that would prevent me from going?"

Luke moved his head side to side, that damned irritation making a muscle flex in his jaw.

"Then having a drink with him won't be a problem?"

"No problem."

He started to turn away but she stopped him. "You have a *personal* problem with this?"

Luke met the question in her eyes. "I don't like the man. He's…" He shrugged. "Sleazy or something."

Her eyes narrowed. "You're right. He is. And I want you to know that this isn't about sex or his money. There's something I have to know about him. That's all I can tell you."

Now his curiosity was really aroused. "You know him from somewhere?"

She glanced at her watch. "Gotta go." She searched his face one last time. "I promise I'll tell you everything later. Right now I have to do this. I'll be back in a couple of hours."

"Whatever."

He watched until she had walked out of her suite before closing the connecting door. There wasn't another personal appearance until seven. Resting his knee was necessary. When Cris got back they could talk some more. As long as she fulfilled her end of their bargain there wasn't a lot he could say.

Worrying about a grown woman who appeared

perfectly capable of taking care of herself was the last thing he should be doing.

But he couldn't help the instinct.

He had a bad feeling about this Sergio character. Maybe he should call his friend Shannon to see what she knew about him. It was Shannon's job to know all there was to know about the high rollers who stayed at her hotel, so Shannon would know if Cris was getting in over her head as Luke suspected.

One quick call would do the job.

CLARISSA TOOK A DEEP BREATH and rapped on the door of room 2514. Her .22 was in an ankle holster, her badge safely hidden in her suite. Even if Fuentes spotted the weapon, it wasn't so unusual for women to carry weapons in this day and age.

The door opened and she fell instantly into character. "Sergio, I was so thrilled to hear from you." She reached up and pressed her cheek to his in a quick, casual greeting.

"Come in, *señora*." He stepped back, gestured broadly with his arm. *"Mi casa es su casa."*

She was in!

"Thank you." She breezed into the room and took a moment to openly admire the opulence. The higher the floor the more lavish the room.

"Wow, this is fantastic." The view out to the Strip was the best she had seen. The room was filled with marble, gold and lots of mirrors. Loads of lush, purple velvet, the sign of royalty.

What these casinos would do to keep their clients happy and feeling generous.

"This is my favorite part." He indicated the massive Jacuzzi tub situated for taking advantage of the spectacular view beyond the balcony. The water was swirling even now as if he was expecting his guest to join him for a relaxing soak.

In his dreams.

She tossed her purse onto the nearest chair. "You mentioned a drink," she reminded him. Getting his mind off the tub and getting naked was her first order of business.

"What is your pleasure, *señora?*" He sauntered toward the massive mahogany bar. His feet were bare. His black trousers most certainly the finest silk. The gray shirt was unbuttoned, the tails hanging free of his trousers in an unspoken invitation.

"White wine." No hard liquor for her; she was on duty.

He smiled and turned around to access the mini wine cellar complete with ornate brass door stationed behind the bar. "You are welcome to peruse the labels. If you do not find one that appeals to you, I will have your request delivered immediately."

No doubt.

"You pick one," Clarissa urged. She wasn't that picky. Chardonnay, Zinfandel, whatever. "Do you come here often?" She leaned against the bar and watched his fluid, confident moves.

"Every three months." He selected a bottle, uncorked it and poured a glass. "And you?"

"This is my first time here at the Free Throw." Which was true, in so far as being a guest. She accepted the stemmed glass of wine. "Thank you."

Fuentes dropped ice into a tumbler and poured himself a bourbon on the rocks. "Ah, so you are a virgin then?"

She laughed softly. "I guess you could say that."

He came around the bar and ushered her to the overstuffed white chairs near the Jacuzzi. "Then I will do my best to see that you are fully satisfied tonight."

She would bet given the chance, he would do exactly that. She sipped her wine and relaxed a little more. "Tell me how it works. This Club Red is something special?"

He inclined his head. "Very special. Private. The club is quite different from the other gambling rooms."

"What do you mean *different?*"

"There are other wagers to be made. Not so much your typical gambling. You will see."

A cell phone chirped. Fuentes removed the phone from his trouser pocket and checked the display. "Pardon," he said in that earthy Spanish accent. "I must take this call. Enjoy your wine and have another if you wish."

He rose from his chair and walked out onto the balcony.

Clarissa sat still exactly three seconds, then she was up and across the room at the bar. She took her time adding more wine to her glass. Not that she had emptied it; she hadn't. But the act gave her reason to leave her seat and survey the room from a better vantage point.

A desk with laptop computer sat only a few feet from the bar. A sofa and the two chairs they had abandoned, along with the hot tub, took up the better part of the room. A huge plasma television hung on the wall above a credenza where papers and a briefcase were placed.

Papers and briefcase first, she decided.

Leaving the bottle of wine on the sleek marble counter, she moved swiftly to the credenza, snagging the television remote en route. As she flipped through the television channels she studied the papers on the table as well as those still lying in his open briefcase.

Lists of numbers. Three columns on each page.

She glanced toward the balcony. Fuentes was still tied up with his call.

Only one option. She sat her glass on the table, visually selected a number and entered the digits into her cell phone as if she were making a call. Then she grabbed her glass, turned away from the television and walked across the room. She closed her phone before a call could attempt to go through.

"I am very sorry for the interruption," Fuentes announced as he entered the room once more.

She tucked her phone back into her pocket. "No problem. I tried to call Luke but, apparently, he's left the room."

Fuentes glanced at the television, probably noting the change in channel. "This husband of yours, is he always so inattentive to your needs?"

Clarissa resumed her seat. The more relaxed this man was in her presence, the more likely she was to have access to his room.

Having a look at his laptop and cell phone would be even better. Technically, any evidence she acquired while in his room was inadmissible. However, since he had invited her into his domain, she could request a warrant based on anything she noticed lying in the open.

"Luke is very busy with his work," she said in defense of her make-believe husband. Fuentes would expect her to defend him to some degree. "I don't always fit into the agenda."

Fuentes assessed her a long moment, from the tips of her bloodred toenails to the top of her mass of unruly auburn curls. "This husband is quite the fool."

Leisurely, she took another sip of her wine. "Do you have any advice on how I should make him pay more attention?" She was pretty sure her host had lots of advice and no small amount of hands-on training he would happily provide.

"I propose that we teach him a lesson." He downed the last of his bourbon. "In my experience a man is more inclined to respect what he is at most risk of losing."

Made sense. In a warped, male-chauvinist way.

"I take it you have a plan?" She moistened her lips. His gaze followed the move.

"Tonight, at the club, we shall show him the way a man properly appreciates his woman."

She sat her glass on the table next to her chair and stood. "Thank you, Sergio. I look forward to tonight."

He rose in that fluid movement that promised power and seduction. "As do I."

Fuentes saw her to the door. As difficult as it proved, Clarissa walked all the way to the stairwell rather than the elevator and descended three levels before stopping. It took every ounce of discipline she possessed to walk, not run.

When she had found a quiet corner, she dug a pen from her purse, then pressed the button that would redial the last number she had entered on her cell phone. She quickly jotted the number on her palm, then hit the end call button. Hitting the proper speed-dial number, she got straight through to Captain Pearson. He wanted kept in the loop of the highest-priority assignments.

"I've made contact with number one." Fuentes was at the very top of their suspect list.

"Excellent," Pearson returned, some amount of relief in his tone.

"I have a number from several pages of numerical lists I discovered in his room," Clarissa explained. "Can you run it for me to see if it's anything relevant? Bank account number? Whatever?"

"Sure."

Clarissa could hear him shuffling the papers on his desk. "Give it to me."

She called off the digits, then listened to him repeat them.

"I'll let you know when I have something for you," her captain promised.

"Thanks." Clarissa closed her phone and slid it back into her pocket.

She still had plenty of time before her next engagement with Luke, but there wasn't a lot she could do relative to her own work other than wait for tonight's grand entrance into Club Red.

Making sure Luke was ready to play the part of *in*attentive husband was probably something she should see to right away. He was being a little overprotective and that could become a problem.

She took the final couple of flights down to the twenty-first floor. After sliding her key card, she pushed into the room.

She was startled to find Luke waiting for her.

In her room, not his.

"We need to talk, Cris," he said.

Uh-oh. That didn't sound good.

She dropped her purse on the desk. "What's up?"

"I talked to Shannon about this Sergio guy and she says you should stay away from him."

Damn.

He could very well have blown her cover.

CHAPTER FIVE

AS EASY AS IT WOULD BE to clear this whole thing up with a simple flash of her badge, Clarissa couldn't do that. She had known from the moment Luke said he was friends with Shannon Bainbridge that telling him her real agenda would be taking a major risk. It was dicey enough that attention had been called to her position at the hotel when he'd decided to propose pretend marriage. But the opportunity had far outweighed the risk.

"I can take care of myself, Luke." She had opted to go the I-am-woman-hear-me-roar route and then cap it off with a guilt trip. "You shouldn't have said anything to Shannon. She could get me in trouble with my boss. You know the rules about fraternization."

The guilt worked. For about ten seconds he seemed truly at a loss for words.

"I'm certain she wouldn't do that behind my back." He plowed his fingers through his hair, giving it that Ty Pennington look. "We've been friends for a really long time."

"So what did she say about Sergio?" Might as well get the dirt while she was at it.

"He has an unsavory reputation with the ladies. She suggested that you avoid him as much as possible."

Clarissa didn't like that new attention had been called to her once more but it was done. If Bainbridge was suspicious of her, Clarissa would pick up on it tonight at Club Red. The lady in charge would definitely be there.

"Don't worry." Clarissa patted Luke on the arm. "I'll be careful."

Right now she wanted to float around the twenty-fifth-floor lounges and see if she could get lucky and run into Russo or Weldon. She'd gotten a glimpse of Russo last night. Intelligence indicated that where one appeared, the other two usually showed up. So far, two had arrived. Weldon should be appearing anytime.

But first she needed a snack to counteract the alcohol. She'd eaten light at lunch. No need to take any chances with her sobriety. Her interest lighting on the fruit bowl, she headed for the bar in her room.

"Cris."

She turned back just in time to see Luke wince with the step he took in her direction.

"Is your knee giving you trouble?" She bit into an apple.

He waved off the question. "I'll live."

Another step, another tightening of his lips.

Nice lips, she realized. Really nice.

He leaned against the counter and watched her take another bite. By the time she took the third chunk out of her apple she had decided he either liked watching her eat or dreaded broaching whatever was on his mind.

"What's your interest in Sergio?" he asked finally.

Since telling him the truth wasn't an option, she went with the story she'd already decided on. "I'm curious about what people with that kind of money do in a place like Club Red."

"Just be careful," he urged. "I know this must all seem very exciting to you—" he grabbed a banana "—but it's like any other lifestyle. It has its up and its downs. Don't let all the glitz in a place like this fool you." He peeled back the yellow skin and took a bite.

She wondered what had given the *Ace* such a careworn attitude about the rich and famous. Maybe he'd endured his own brand of painful reality as a celebrity. Well, she had already witnessed one drawback for him—the ladies. Though, admittedly, most men didn't seem to consider that a problem.

Somehow, Clarissa got the feeling that the *Ace* here had a major problem with this skin-deep kind of attention. The idea made her curious but she didn't have time for indulging herself.

"That's cute," she said before she could recall the words.

He frowned. "What's cute?"

Well, she'd done it now. "The whole protector thing. I can't remember the last time a guy bothered." Not exactly a flattering admission, but there it was.

Luke reached up, touched a long, loopy curl that had fallen loose from the clasp holding the wild mane from her face. "You have the most gorgeous hair. I've never seen anything like it. It's like fire, but soft and…I don't know…alluring."

Heat sped through her veins as her gaze connected with those deep brown eyes of his. "Are you flirting with me, Mr. Jennings?"

The hint of a smile quirked his lips. "I guess I am." He slid his fingertips down the length of that strand before straightening away from the counter. "I'll see you at seven, then."

"Yeah…seven."

Clarissa admired his fine backside again as he made his way back to his own side of the connecting door and her heart did one of those silly little somersaults.

Being attracted to him was such a waste of energy at the moment. This was not the time for such foolish fantasies.

She had to remember that Luke Jennings had several strikes against him. He was a professional athlete. A celebrity. Not exactly good boyfriend material…much less husband stock.

Good thing they were only pretending to be married.

Inspiration struck.

Maybe they could have pretend sex.

Oh, she was bad.

10:00 p.m.

LUKE DIDN'T LIKE THIS AT ALL.

Club Red was dark and exclusive. A pair of intense poker games were underway, but a lot of the action was taking place in small private rooms, each guarded by a big, burly member of security. Shannon drifted around the room ensuring the guests had everything they needed.

Luke was concerned that Cris was right about

his mentioning the business with Fuentes being a mistake. Shannon had been watching Cris's every move since their arrival an hour ago. If his big mouth got her into trouble, he would really feel like a jerk.

Cris looked amazing in the jade dress. Tiny spaghetti straps. Sleek satin. Gorgeous. The instant the personal shopper had shown it to him he had known the dress was perfect for her.

Every male in the room had stared at her when she entered the posh club on his arm. Something like pride had welled inside him. He'd been feeling a few other swelling sensations, as well.

She had given him orders to back off on the whole worrying-about-her thing.

Where the hell was she going now?

The corridor that led to the restrooms. He probably would have figured she was heading to the ladies' room if he hadn't seen Fuentes go in that direction just a minute or so before.

If she wasn't back in five minutes Luke was going in.

For her own good.

FUENTES HAD FOLLOWED Russo into the ladies' room.

Clarissa hesitated at the door. She could

walk in and no one would think a thing about it…couldn't she?

Damn straight.

She removed her shoes and, holding her breath, she pushed the door inward and held on to it to force it to close quietly.

Listening intently, she located her two suspects. They had gone beyond the small lobby area and into one of the stalls. Moving soundlessly on bare feet, she made her way in that direction. Elegant stalls, built like small closets with full-length doors, lined one wall while marble counters lined the other. Fresh rose petals decorated the counters around each sink. Gilded mirrors and ornate soap dispensers completed the luxurious decorating.

Careful to keep her movements silent, Clarissa slipped into the stall next to the one where things were heating up between Russo and Fuentes. The sounds of their frantic sex allowed Clarissa to gently close the door of her stall.

Simultaneous climaxes were punctuated by grunts and moans. She hoped coming in here wasn't going to accomplish anything more than a few seconds of voyeurism.

"You placed the order?" Russo wanted to know.

The whir of a zipper followed by, "Of course."

"Three days, Sergio. If there are any mistakes this time, we'll be looking for another partner."

Clarissa's heart burst into a frantic race. Gotcha! These two were definitely working together. Now if she could only connect Weldon and find out exactly what the goods being handled were.

"I have the list and the order is taken care of," he murmured severely. "The first shipment will arrive in three days. You need not worry, woman."

"Shannon told me you had a new friend."

"What of it?"

"Inviting her here is very risky. I would hate to see your libido get you killed, Sergio. I'm sure you recall what happened with the last one."

Clarissa's pulse thumped. Her interaction with Fuentes had been noticed. And Shannon had definitely had something to do with outing her.

That certainly drove another nail in the woman's coffin. Luke was going to be very disappointed in his friend.

"I will handle this one more carefully," Sergio said without the slightest hint of humility.

The door to the stall they shared opened.

Clarissa tensed.

"I hope so," Russo said, her tone pointed.

"Stay out of my personal business, woman. You are not in charge."

Who was in charge? Clarissa would really like to know the answer to that.

Water running muffled their voices. She heard snippets. Something about *moving forward*. And *three months*.

Was this business they conducted done on a quarterly basis? Fuentes had said he came here every three months.

When the main door whooshed closed behind them, Clarissa dared to slip out of her stall. She moved to the door and hesitated. Going back out immediately wouldn't be a good idea. Anyone noticing her exit from the corridor would know she had been in here at the same time as the other two.

She would wait.

The minutes dragged past like hours. Luke was probably wondering where she was.

Three minutes. That should be long enough.

First, she eased the door open one millimeter at a time until the slightest crack appeared, allowing her to see into the corridor.

The air evacuated her lungs.

A man waited in the dimly lit hall, not ten feet from the door.

Weldon.

Slowly, a millimeter, then two…until the crack disappeared, she closed the door.

Damn it.

His being out there could be coincidence but how could she take the chance that it wasn't?

She couldn't.

A distraction was the only way to get out of here and even then it might not work.

Moving away from the door, she tugged her cell phone from her purse and entered Luke's number. She would have some explaining to do later, but right now the important thing was getting out of here.

"I need your help," she said.

The concern in his voice sent another of those ridiculous giddy feelings surging through her. She was not accustomed to enjoying the whole macho-guy thing. This whirlwind assignment had evidently affected her equilibrium, certainly her good sense.

"There's a man in the corridor outside the ladies' room. I need you to distract him so I can get out without his knowing I was in here."

His silence told her that her request sounded just as bizarre to him as it did to her, perhaps more. But there was no help for it.

"I'll take care of it," Luke finally replied.

She put her phone away, moved back to the door and eased it open once more in those infinitesimal degrees. Luke's voice announced that he had arrived to do his part. Weldon turned toward him, his back to her position now.

"You have a light?" Luke asked, a cigar tucked between his lips.

Weldon dug a lighter from the pocket of his elegant trousers and mumbled something about there being complimentary matches available.

Now or never. Clarissa pulled the door open far enough to slide out. She couldn't head back toward the main room since Weldon was facing that direction and there was no place for her to have come from except the restroom.

If he glanced over his shoulder he would see her. She had to move.

Men's room.

There was no other choice.

Clarissa walked backward, one step, then two.

Luke, thank God, kept his attention glued to Weldon. If he glanced her way, even briefly, Weldon would know someone was behind him.

Her fingers found the door frame. She eased closer and pressed against the door with her full body weight.

Don't let him look back.

She pushed into the men's room and let the door close in the same manner as she had the door to the ladies' room, slowly, silently.

Once the door was closed, she sucked in a deep breath. She braced her forehead against the door and let the tension drain to a more tolerable level.

Close. Too damned close.

The door moved.

She stumbled back.

Luke pushed into the room.

Relief made her knees weak.

"What're you doing?" she whispered. He was supposed to distract Weldon, not follow her.

"I told him someone was waiting for me." He moved away from the door, forcing her to take a few more steps backward. "How else were you going to explain being in here?"

"You were supposed to distract him," she muttered.

He shrugged those silk-clad shoulders. "The man wasn't going anywhere. Absently, he's waiting for someone." That he said this with a pointed look at her warned he understood she was the someone.

Might as well acknowledge his stellar move. "Good save."

"Now." He stepped directly into her personal space. "How about telling me what this is all about."

The door opened.

Her gaze collided with Luke's.

There was only one thing to do.

She grabbed him and kissed him hard on the mouth.

He pulled her body into his, and then everything else vanished.

Time. Place. Whoever the hell had walked into the men's room. All of it melted away.

There was nothing but the feel of his lips on hers.

CHAPTER SIX

LUKE COULDN'T HIDE what she was doing to him. Whoever had entered the room didn't matter. It only mattered that he could feel every contour of her body pressed against his. The taste of her lips, like white wine and hot female, was driving him out of his mind. Her arms were around his neck, her fingers prowling restlessly through his hair.

He wanted more than just this kiss…more than this erection caused by her touch and her taste.

She drew back just enough to catch her breath. "Sorry about that," she murmured.

His tongue slid out to savor the taste of her on his lips. "Don't be."

A toilet flushed and his head snapped up.

"We should get out of here," she whispered, the words urgent.

He wrapped his fingers around her hand and led her out of the male domain. He didn't stop until they were back in the main gaming room.

"I need a drink." As much to brace himself as to wet his throat. That kiss had done a number on his head.

She nodded. "Me, too."

He had some serious questions for her, but those would have to wait until they were in neutral territory. Definitely not here. And not now.

"Scotch," he told the bartender.

"Wine," she said in response to his glance in her direction.

With the drinks in hand, they mingled amid the crowd a moment, then settled in a less populated area of the room.

"You okay?"

She took a hefty swallow from her glass and nodded. "I'm okay."

"We'll need to talk about that later," he said.

"Yeah."

She agreed but didn't look at him.

He liked that she wore her hair down tonight. The luscious red mane draped her shoulders in sexy waves that begged to be touched. When they were kissing, he'd been too busy enjoying the sensual landscape of her body to think about her hair.

Next time.

"I…" She glanced up at him. "I have to talk to someone."

Before he could respond she had darted into the crowd. He wasn't the least bit surprised when she cozied up to Fuentes.

What the hell was going on with this lady?

CLARISSA WOULDN'T BE getting out of some direct questions from Luke later, but right now she had a job to do and he would just have to deal with it.

"Ah, *señora,* I wondered where you had gotten to," Fuentes said as he draped an arm around her waist.

Clarissa could still smell Russo's perfume on his shirt.

"I had to take care of my husband." She smiled, let him assume what he would.

"We all have our obligations," Fuentes said with a glance at Russo. "Sometimes pleasant, sometimes not."

Sounded like Fuentes was tired of some of his.

"That's all the more reason to take the good times whenever you can, wherever you can," Clarissa suggested.

"Yes." He settled that dark gaze on her. "You are so right, Cris."

Clarissa noticed Shannon Bainbridge watching her. The woman hardly made it difficult.

"I think there are some in the room who don't

like our new friendship," Clarissa said frankly. Might as well push the envelope and see if she could get an invitation to the man's suite again.

"Perhaps you would like to join me for a more private drink." He shot a sidelong look at Luke, who lounged at the bar. "We were going to give your foolish husband a lesson in appreciation."

"I thought you'd never ask."

Fuentes took her hand. "Then let us go."

"Wait." When he'd met her eyes once more, she said, "I never did get to see how the private booths work." She gestured to the closed doors on the other side of the room. "You promised to show me *everything*."

Fuentes grinned. "I would not want you to miss this, *señora*."

He led her to an unoccupied booth, ushered her inside, then closed the door, separating them from the crowded room. "There is not so much to see."

Nothing but a table and chair and a laptop computer.

"You press this button—" he indicated a red button on the table "—if you require assistance or service."

"What kind of gambling is done like this?" She gestured to the laptop. "I don't see the fun in this."

He wrapped his arms around her waist and

pulled her backside against his pelvis. He was hard already. She resisted the impulse to shudder in disgust.

"Here, *señora,* you can order anything your heart desires. *Anything.*"

Amping up the risk, she turned in his arms and peered up at him. "I'm ready for that private drink now."

He held her gaze a long moment, backing out of the embrace. She followed him from the club without sparing a glance in Luke's direction. She didn't want to see the question on his face. The explanations would have to come later.

They took the elevator down one floor. By the time they reached his room, his hold on her hand had become a crushing vise.

"What is your pleasure?" he asked as soon as they were beyond his closed door. He tossed his room key onto the nearest table and shouldered out of his jacket and tossed it aside. "Wine?"

"Yes." She surveyed his room, noting the papers were gone. Probably packed away in the briefcase that still sat on the credenza. The laptop was closed. He must have realized how irresponsible he'd been leaving his documents lying about so carelessly.

He arrived at her side with the stemmed glass in hand. She accepted the drink. "Thank you."

After a long swallow of his whiskey, he wiped his mouth and set his gaze on hers. "If we hurry, we could enjoy each other before your husband becomes too annoyed and comes to collect you."

Clarissa wasn't sure Luke would come at all. She knew how leaving with Fuentes must have looked to him. There was a possibility he would insist on backing off on the whole pretend marriage. That wasn't a problem really—in a few hours it would be over, anyway. And she had her in.

But the bereft feeling that speared through her at the thought refuted her every assertion, startling her. Oh, come on! What was wrong with her here?

"You're right," she said to Fuentes. "But…" She moved in close to him. "When we have sex, I don't want to hurry. I want it slow and thorough."

He kissed her. Supreme willpower was required for her to react as he would expect when gagging was her first and strongest impulse.

Drawing back, he murmured, "I have something for you."

A forced smile pushed up the corners of her mouth. "I love surprises."

"Don't move," he ordered.

When he disappeared into the adjoining bedroom, she went straight for his jacket. His cell phone was in the interior pocket. Praying he wouldn't come back into the room and catch her, she synchronized their phones and sent the top five numbers stored in his to hers. She had barely gotten the phone closed and tucked back into his pocket when she heard him coming.

She pressed her phone to her ear and rushed back to the middle of the room where she had been standing when he'd disappeared into the bedroom. "I promise," she whispered, forcing annoyance into her tone as she carried on the one-sided conversation. "Yes."

Huffing in frustration, she shoved the phone into her purse. "He ordered me back to our suite."

"First," Fuentes said, "you must have this."

He gave her a long, narrow, velvet box.

Velvet meant jewels.

She shook her head. "I can't accept this."

"Accept it," he insisted. "Or I will be mortally wounded."

She opened the box and gasped at the diamond bracelet. "Sergio, this is—"

"Yours."

He took the bracelet from the box and fastened it around her wrist. "Now go. Take care of your husband. I have some business to attend to. Perhaps we may have breakfast in the morning."

Those dark eyes bored into hers. "Here. In private. Where we will have all the time we need."

She tiptoed to reach his cheek and kissed him. The approval in his expression told her she'd made the right move.

He placed the key to his room in her hand. "I'll be waiting."

She nodded, then rushed toward the door.

"Sweet dreams," he called out behind her.

Clarissa didn't look back. She exited his room and hurried down the four flights to the twenty-first floor. She didn't know if Luke would be back at the room, but she needed to check in with Pearson and see if he had anything on that number yet.

She'd just tucked her key card into the door slot when her cell phone vibrated. That was something else she needed to do—send those five phone numbers to Pearson.

Speaking of which, he was her caller. Working more overtime.

"Rivers," she said in greeting.

"I found something on that number."

"Let me get into my room."

He paused while she unlocked her door and pushed into the room. She kicked off her shoes. "Okay, give it to me."

"It's a serial number for a weapon."

The image of those columns of numbers on the pages in Fuentes's briefcase flashed through her mind.

"Handguns?"

"Worse. Military weapons. This is now officially a federal case, Rivers. We're going to need to call in ATF to take control."

Clarissa blinked, the reality penetrating the final layer of cognitive processes.

Weapons. Stolen. Probably the shipment he had guaranteed Russo would be delivered in three days.

"Does that mean I'm off the case?" Her heart rammed against her ribs as she waited for his response. She hated like hell to get this close to a case and then have to back off because it became federal jurisdiction. Especially after LVMPD had done all the grunt work.

"You stay put until I tell you different."

More of that bone-weakening relief she had been experiencing tonight.

"Just one thing," Pearson instructed.

"Yes, sir?"

"Keep you head low, Rivers. This one may get ugly."

"Don't worry, Cap, I've got it under control.

I've got some telephone numbers to send you. Check your e-mail."

"Do I want to know how you got those numbers?"

"Nope."

"Send 'em."

Clarissa ended the call and quickly went through the numbers, sending each one to Pearson's inbox. As she sent the final number, the connecting door between her suite and Luke's burst inward. He strode into the room, anger radiating from every square inch of his tall, athletic body. No amount of silk could disguise it.

She had a feeling Pearson was more right than he knew.

Hell was about to break loose.

CHAPTER SEVEN

"OKAY, MAYBE I AM OVERREACTING," Luke agreed, his fury refusing to abate. "But one minute you've got me rescuing you from the restroom where some guy is waiting or watching…" He threw up his hands. "I don't know. Then you disappear with Fuentes." His glare fixed on her then. "What's going on, Cris?"

She stopped pacing and faced him, her green eyes glittering, the mass of fiery hair flowing around her shoulders. "My name is Clarissa Rivers."

Clarissa? Cris. Okay, he could see that.

"Cris is a nickname."

She nodded. "I'm a cop."

Luke laughed. Couldn't help himself. But the amusement fizzled with her continued glare.

"Las Vegas Metro." She reached beneath the cushion of the sofa and pulled out a badge. "See for yourself." She tossed it to him.

Looked real enough. But this was Vegas, where anything was possible.

He placed the badge on the table next to the sofa. "Why would a cop be working as a maid in a Casino hotel?"

"I'm undercover." She moistened her lips, looked a little hesitant. "That's all I can tell you right now.'

Like she was getting off that easy. "If you're a cop—" he tugged off his jacket and pitched it onto the sofa "—then why doesn't Shannon know?" Shannon was the VIP manager. She would know everything that was going down in her hotel.

"Shannon can't know who I am or what I'm doing. Is that clear?"

A frown furrowed his brow, making his head ache to match his painful bum knee. "Is she a suspect?" That was impossible. Shannon was Shannon. A straight shooter. A great pal. She didn't even drink.

"I'm sorry, Luke. I can't give you any more than that. But I can tell you that if you breathe a word about this to anyone, you could endanger my operation as well as my life."

The words shook him even as on some level he understood that would be the case. "So Fuentes and that guy in the corridor upstairs are both suspects?"

"Like I said," she reiterated, "I can't tell you any more."

One of those tiny straps fell down her shoulder, making him want to follow its path with his mouth. At least now he knew for sure that kiss hadn't been real.

"So that kiss in the men's room," he ventured, clearly a glutton for punishment, "it was part of your cover?"

She looked directly into his eyes, something in hers changed. "Yes."

Before he could stutter out some reply, she walked straight up to him. "But this—" she put her arms around his neck "—this isn't about work."

Then she kissed him. Slower, with far more attention to detail. Deep, lingering, mind-blowing kisses. His hands found their way to her hair. Soft, silky. He could touch her like this forever.

She undid his shirt, one button at a time. Then she pulled the tails from his trousers. He shuddered with the anticipation burning through his veins.

He wanted…he wanted to undress her but she was in control. She pushed his hands away so that she could shove his shirt off his shoulders. Every move of her hands was accompanied by her forcing him back another step.

"Cuff links," he mumbled between the tangling of their lips.

He helped her remove the cuff links, and his shirt dropped to the floor. She forced him back another step. His hands found their way to the delicate zipper of her dress. Down, down, down, he pushed it. Then he slid the garment in that same direction. She stepped out of it, leaving it a glimmering jade mass against the white carpet. His gaze slid back down her thighs to the weapon strapped there. Before he could comment, she forced him back yet another step.

His hands skimmed her body. Bra…panties. God, she was nearly naked. He drew back to look…trembled at her beauty. The next step landed him against the door frame of the opening that connected their rooms.

She scratched her side. That was when he noticed the scattering of red blotches.

"Hives—from the maid's uniform. It's a long story. Now," she said as she wrenched his trousers open, "do you have condoms, Luke?"

He nodded.

The trousers fell to his ankles.

"Mmm." She surveyed his body, her gaze landing on the tented front of his boxers.

He toed off his shoes and stumbled free of his

trousers. She was guiding him into his room…toward the bed. Good thing because he couldn't take his eyes off her even for a second.

By the time the backs of his knees encountered the mattress his boxers were history and her bra was slipping off her arms.

Her breasts were perfect, just the right size and with an intriguing upward tilt as if the nipples were designed just for him to enjoy with his mouth.

She pushed him down onto the bed and straddled his waist. "Condoms?"

He reached blindly into the drawer of the table next to the bed. Her lips were teasing his…nibbling…licking and promising things that made his heart thud.

Not relinquishing control, she tugged the condom from his hand and tore it open. His fingers fisted in the linens. She moved backward on her knees until his erection stood firmly in front of her. His breath caught as her cool fingers worked the condom into place.

Then she dropped onto the mattress next to him and said, "Your turn."

Stunned for a few moments, he could only lie there with her sighing like a kitten next to him. Then he bolted into action.

CLARISSA'S BREATH CAUGHT at the sight of him looming over her, his weight resting on his knees. She loved watching him hesitate. The idea that he couldn't decide where to put his hands first made her feel a heady rush of power. Then he touched her. His hands glided up her torso and closed around her breasts. She made a sound of approval. He leaned lower, kissed one breast, then the other. As he kissed his way up her throat, one hand pushed inside her panties.

She was hot and wet and his searching fingers found all the right spots. She arched against his hand, wanting more.

He groaned.

She stilled.

Not a sound indicating pleasure.

But he didn't stop teasing her intimately.

Then she realized. His knee. His weight was resting on his knees.

She pressed her palms against his chest in a gesture of stop. When his questioning gaze lit on hers, she said, "I want back on top."

Confusion reigned a moment before understanding dawned. "I'm not an invalid," he growled.

"Luke—"

While he dragged her panties downward, she lifted her bottom, then her legs, off the mattress to accommodate his efforts. The silk thong slid off her feet and landed on the floor.

"Spread your legs," he ordered.

Okay, so he wanted to be in charge now.

Fine.

She did as he ordered. For several long seconds he did nothing but look. The longer he looked, the hotter she got. Her body started to writhe in anticipation.

"Luke," she warned.

Then he shifted into position between her legs. His tightly compressed lips told her how much every move cost him.

His mouth closed over hers and her hands found their way to his chest…his back. She wanted to touch all of him. To feel his weight on hers.

He lifted her hips. She reached for him, guided him into position. And then he entered her in one deliberate thrust.

They both held perfectly still for several frantic beats of her heart. It felt so good to have him inside her, filling her, making her ache to move.

He started that ancient rhythm and all thought ceased. There was only their bodies, joined in complement. The sensations climbed and climbed until she couldn't hold back any longer. She came with a vengeance. He tumbled into climax right after her.

Seconds later he lay next to her, both of them gasping for breath.

Before she caught her breath completely, she reached into the drawer for another condom. He removed the first and she quickly replaced it.

"Don't even think about moving," she warned as she climbed astride him. "It's my turn."

She sank onto him in one slow, delicious effort.

Clarissa didn't wait for her body to adjust to the new depth, she just began to rock. His hands closed around her breasts as she kept up the steady movements, pausing now and then to grind against him. His fingers clamped onto her thighs while his face contorted with euphoria.

When the first signs of quickening hit her, she sped up her pace. Attuned to her needs, he lifted his hips to increase the pressure. She cried out at the incredible sensation.

They crashed into release together for a second time. She slumped onto his chest, couldn't bear the idea of disengaging their bodies.

For long minutes they lay that way without saying a word, their respiration struggling to return to normal. Then she couldn't wait any longer.

"Tell me about your knee."

She felt the stillness overtake him.

Propping her arms on his muscular chest, she rested her head in her hands. "Tell me," she pressed.

His eyes searched hers, maybe for some hidden agenda. But she had none. She genuinely wanted to know.

"It's wrecked. There will be no more races for me."

His statement sent shockwaves quaking through her.

"Besides my doctor and my agent," he went on, "you're the only person on the planet who knows this."

She kissed his lips. "I guess you'll have no choice but to kill me now."

He laughed in spite of himself.

"So." She turned serious again. "What's your plan?"

He exhaled a weary breath. "Keep doing endorsements as long as someone will have me and, after that, I don't know."

What a terrible feeling that had to be. He had clearly worked long and hard to reach this place in his chosen pursuit and now it was gone. All he'd worked for. Damn, that was ugly.

"There are other things you could do," she suggested. "Coaching."

"Yeah." He toyed with a strand of her hair. "I thought about that."

She traced the angular line of his jaw. "I think you would make a great coach."

"Believe it or not, I have a teaching degree," he confessed, almost self-consciously.

"Teaching. That's great. Good teachers are always in demand." She scooted up to put her eyes directly in line with his. "See, you have lots of options."

"No feeling sorry for myself?"

She shook her head. "Absolutely not."

"What about you?" He rolled her onto her back and burrowed between her legs, resting most of his weight on his elbows on either side of her. "What made you decide to be a cop?"

She wrapped her legs around his and teased the erection that hadn't sagged in the slightest. "My father was a financial mogul. Big bucks. Never enough time for his only daughter." She left out the part about the nannies and maids and numerous wives.

"No wonder you seemed so at home in this world." He kissed the tip of her nose. "Is your father still alive?"

She nodded. "Living on his own Caribbean island with wife number six." Oops, she hadn't meant to say that last part.

"What happened to your mother?"

"She died when I was two. A car crash. I don't even remember her."

"I'm sorry." He kissed her lips. "That's tough."

She glanced at the clock on the bedside table. "I have to go back up there."

"It's after midnight," Luke noted, surprised or maybe disappointed that she would even suggest leaving the bed.

"Which means it's technically Saturday morning. I have to try to close this case in the next twenty-four hours. I know you don't understand, but I have my orders."

He heaved a sigh. "I guess a cop can't be expected to work nine to five."

She smiled. "Chaos would own the night if we did."

He flopped back onto the mattress, freeing her. "Just remember, when you're done, I'll be waiting here for an encore."

"Deal." She scooted off the bed and grabbed for her panties.

"Is what you're about to do dangerous?" he asked as he went up on his side and propped his head in his hand.

She couldn't stop herself. She had to survey

that long, lean body. "Possibly." She licked her lips. God, he was gorgeous.

And nice for a celebrity…and a professional athlete.

"Maybe I should go as your backup," he suggested all too sincerely.

"You stay here," she ordered, her tone leaving no room for argument. "The last thing I need is to have to worry about your safety."

"Just be careful," he urged. "I'd kind of like to get to know you better."

Clarissa smiled. Sweet. She rushed over and gave him a quick kiss on the forehead. "We'll talk about this later." She backed away from the bed. "For sure."

CHAPTER EIGHT

1:30 a.m.

CLARISSA TUGGED AT HER DRESS as she stepped off the elevator on the twenty-fifth floor. She scratched her side. Damned hives. They should be gone by now.

"Back for more, Mrs. Jennings?" Douglas asked as she entered.

Clarissa smiled. "For a little while." She glanced around the room. "I was looking for Mr. Fuentes."

If he was here…maybe she could get another look at those numerical lists in his room. She had the key, after all. She couldn't take anything and expect it to be admissible in court, but she could get as much information as possible in hopes of heading off wherever those weapons were going. Terrorists most likely. In that event, even without a warrant the information might be usable.

"One moment, ma'am." Douglas spoke to someone via his Secret Service–type communications link, then he turned to her. "Mr. Fuentes is upstairs in Club Red."

She gifted the security guard with a big smile. "Thank you, Douglas."

In deference to her stilettos and her aching feet, she took the elevator. She strode into the corridor and headed for the door. Another security guard nodded as she entered the room.

She glanced around the room. "Mr. Fuentes?" she asked.

"Booth two," the guard told her.

Clarissa started forward, then hesitated. "Oh, my." She checked her purse. "I forgot my cell." She smiled broadly for the guard and to hide the lie. "I'll be right back."

This time she took the stairs. Moving as fast as she dared, she rushed to room 2514. With a quick glance right, then left, she slid the key card into the slot and pushed into the room. The bright neon glow from the Strip pouring into the wall of windows prevented the room from being pitch black.

After snagging her .22 from her thigh holster, she moved quickly to the credenza and opened the briefcase. Scanning the room once more, she dared to turn on the floor lamp next to her. The lists were there. She flipped through the pages hoping to find a name or a location. Then she found it. Miami.

So Russo was the delivery connection. The weapons would be shipped to Miami and then distributed to the black-market buyers from there.

How did Weldon fit into the picture?

Clarissa dug out her cell phone and put through the call to Pearson. "Miami's the distribution point," she told him. "Based on what I overheard earlier tonight, I'd say three days from now is the date."

"I'll pass this along to ATF," Pearson said. "Any luck connecting Bainbridge to this operation?"

Clarissa actually hoped that there wouldn't be a connection, since Luke considered her a friend.

Luke.

Damn. How had she let that happen?

I'd kind of like to get to know you better.

"Not yet," she said in answer to Pearson's question. She couldn't let thoughts of Luke distract her just now. "I should get out of here."

"I don't have to remind you," Pearson said, "that we need this case closed ASAP."

"Yes, sir."

She closed the phone. Time to make her exit.

Her weapon still clenched in her right hand, her purse and phone in her left, she was halfway across the room when she heard someone outside the door.

Damn.

With no time for second thoughts, she dove into plan B. Or out of it as the case might be. She jerked the zipper of her dress down far enough to allow it to puddle on the floor. Stepping out of the mound of fabric, she hit the call key on her cell twice to put another call through to Pearson. She ripped off the thigh holster, dropped it, the weapon, her purse and phone into the mountain of satin. The best she could hope for was that Pearson would either hear what was to come, or he would assume something was wrong when she didn't respond.

If she were lucky he would send help…fast.

She straightened just in time for the door to open.

The lights came on and Fuentes stopped abruptly, his gaze landing on her, the door still open and resting against his hand.

Clarissa trailed the fingers of her right hand down her abdomen. "I've been waiting for you."

The look of disappointment on Fuentes's face wasn't what she had been going for.

When Rita Russo and Mark Weldon entered the room behind him, she understood why.

She was made.

LUKE DIDN'T LIKE THIS one little bit. Maybe he was a washed-up cyclist and maybe he didn't know the first damned thing about undercover work, but he did know a dangerous situation when faced with one.

Cris…Clarissa was on her own. *That* was dangerous.

He stuffed his feet into his shoes. He was dressed; there wasn't any reason for him not to go up there, too. He wouldn't get in her way.

He could just be handy in case she needed him.

Decision made, he was out the door and headed for the elevator.

On the twenty-fifth floor, he checked with Douglas. According to the security guard, Mrs. Jennings had gone up to Club Red about thirty minutes prior. Luke headed up one floor, sticking with the elevator, considering his aching knee.

He'd spent the last half hour replaying those moments when they had been making love, and he had to say he had never met anyone who made him feel the way Clarissa did. He did not want to lose her. She didn't care about his soon-to-be-history celebrity status or his money. He liked that a lot.

He liked *her*.

No way was he going to hang back when she could be in danger.

The security guard at Club Red insisted that Mrs. Jennings was not there. She had come, yes, but she had left to get her cell phone.

Luke knew that wasn't correct because she'd had her phone when she left the room.

Something had to be wrong.

He spotted his friend Shannon. Clarissa didn't trust Shannon, but she was Luke's friend. And he was desperate. He was certain she could help.

CLARISSA IGNORED RUSSO'S GLARE and Weldon's leer. It was Fuentes's hard stare that concerned her the most. His ego would be bruised. Never a good thing for a woman in her position.

"I told you," Russo snarled. "You're a fool, Fuentes. She's a goddamned cop."

Weldon finally shifted his attention from her. "We can't push her over the balcony from this room."

Now there was a unique idea. "If anyone goes over the balcony," Clarissa said, speaking louder than necessary for Pearson's benefit, "it'll be you, Weldon."

Russo pointed her furious glare at Fuentes. "You screwed up, you take care of her."

The last thing Clarissa wanted was for those two to get away. If they walked out of this room, they could be out of Vegas before LVMPD had time to respond.

"Actually," Clarissa said, going for broke, "I'm afraid I'm a problem for all three of you."

Weldon's gaze narrowed, as did Russo's.

"What the hell is she talking about?" Weldon demanded of Fuentes.

"I'm afraid he's as in the dark as the two of you," Clarissa warned. "You see, I'm not just a cop. I'm ATF. Backup is in the hotel. I would suggest that the three of you start working out a strategy for cooperating. Unless, of course, you want to do time in a federal prison."

She held her ground, didn't flinch while the three obviously considered her words.

"If she had backup," Fuentes finally spoke up, "she wouldn't be standing here like this." He gestured to her mostly naked body. "She's bluffing."

Well, thank you, Sergio.

"I'm not bluffing," she countered.

A rap on the door drew everyone's attention there.

Fuentes checked the security peep hole. He glanced at Clarissa before opening the door.

She knew it was far too soon for LVMPD to have arrived.

Shannon Bainbridge joined the crowd. At least Clarissa had her answer about Bainbridge.

Clarissa's triumphant feeling wilted when Luke Jennings stepped into the room after the woman he thought was his friend.

Her heart dropped all the way to her stilettos.

Their gazes locked and Clarissa recognized the fear in his. Not for himself, but for her. The realization squeezed her heart.

"I'm sorry, Mr. Fuentes," Bainbridge said. "I just learned that Miss Rivers is LVMPD." She glanced at Luke. "And I'm afraid Mr. Jennings knows far too much."

The shock in Luke's face deepened the regret Clarissa felt. She was trained for this kind of thing. He was ill prepared and undeserving of the fate these four surely had in mind for the two of them.

"Can I put my dress back on now?" Clarissa demanded, drawing the focus back to her. Her plan was damned thin but she had to do something. She could not let her operation get an innocent civilian killed.

She couldn't let Luke get hurt.

"Step away from the dress," Fuentes ordered. He reached beneath his jacket and removed a weapon.

Well, there went that plan.

"Luke is upset about his damaged knee," Bainbridge piped up. "His career is over. No one would be surprised if he turned suicidal." Her gaze landed on Clarissa. "And took the new woman in his life with him."

"You'll pay for this, Shannon," Luke snarled, his fury blazing past the shock.

"Excellent idea, Shannon," Russo said. "Weldon and I will take Luke back down to his room. You and Shannon," she said to Fuentes, "bring her down in another minute or so. Going in such a large group might draw suspicion."

At least they weren't going to die here and now. That was something.

Each added minute provided opportunity.

"I am armed, Jennings," Weldon cautioned as he patted his jacket. "One unexpected move and you're dead."

Luke didn't answer the man, and he didn't take his eyes off Clarissa until Weldon had pushed him out the door.

Fuentes approached Clarissa with extreme caution. He picked up her dress. Her .22, purse and phone remained on the white carpet. He toed the weapon over to Shannon, then stomped the phone.

Clarissa hoped Pearson had figured out something was wrong.

"Put the dress back on," Fuentes ordered.

Since she didn't want Luke out of her sight too long, Clarissa made quick work of obeying this jerk's order. When her dress was zipped, Fuentes ushered her out of the room. Bainbridge, the .22 hidden in her jacket pocket, followed.

"We'll take the stairs," Fuentes commanded. "I don't want to risk running into anyone in the elevator."

Suited Clarissa. More of that time and opportunity.

As they moved down the first flight, Fuentes kept his right hand clamped around her left arm. The weapon was in his left. She knew from the way he'd zipped her dress and poured her drinks that he was right handed. Good.

Bainbridge was directly behind them. Clarissa was banking on the idea that she wasn't in the habit of shooting people.

One...two...

"Three!" Her right hand manacling the rail, Clarissa shoved her weight into Fuentes as they hit the first step on the next set of stairs.

Fuentes regained his balance, but Clarissa was prepared for that. She clamped down on his arm with her teeth and rammed harder into him with her trunk at the same time.

This time he stumbled. Clarissa's arm twisted

but she didn't let go of the railing. Fuentes took several strands of her hair with him as he stumbled down the stairs. His weapon discharged, the explosion deafening.

Bainbridge rushed toward Clarissa.

Clarissa stuck out her foot in the woman's path and gave her a push, sending her tumbling after Fuentes.

Kicking off her stilettos, Clarissa ran back the way they had come. She banged on the first door she reached and shouted, "Call the police!"

She skidded to a stop at the elevator, stabbed the call button, then banged on a nearby door and screamed for help again.

The elevator doors opened and the car was filled to capacity with...of all things...cheerleaders.

LUKE STOOD IN THE MIDDLE of his room, Weldon's handgun aimed at him. Russo was on her cell phone attempting to call Fuentes since he hadn't shown up with Clarissa yet.

She had to be all right. Luke wouldn't believe anything else. He couldn't lose her now; he had only just found her.

"Something's wrong," Russo said. She glanced at Weldon. "Get rid of him. I'm going to find Fuentes."

Russo opened the door and Clarissa barged in.

"Drop the weapon," Clarissa ordered.

Russo looked her up and down, then scoffed since Clarissa was unarmed. "Where's Fuentes?"

"He's lying at the bottom of the stairs," Clarissa said, "with his friend Bainbridge. Hopefully with a broken leg or neck." She shrugged. "Or whatever. A whole precinct of LVMPD cops are on their way up." She looked from Russo to Weldon. "Now would be a good time to give up."

"Get out of my way," Russo ordered.

Clarissa shook her head. "I wouldn't go out there if I were you."

Weldon stormed over to the door. "I'm getting out of here," he announced.

"There are about a hundred cheerleaders out there," Clarissa warned. "They've formed a human barrier and unless you're prepared to shoot them all, I would suggest you figure out a way to cut a deal." Clarissa looked from one to the other. "After all, you two are just middlemen. You know ATF is going to want bigger fish."

Weldon and Russo exchanged a look.

"LVMPD!"

The door burst open and the room was suddenly full of cops dressed in SWAT gear.

Luke crumpled into the closest chair.

They were safe.

His gaze settled on Clarissa.

She had saved his life.

And he had almost gotten her killed by trusting the wrong person.

4:00 a.m.

CLARISSA'S CASE WAS CLOSED more than twenty-four hours early. That had to make her the winner of the bet, head start not withstanding.

Russo and Weldon were spilling their guts. Bainbridge and Fuentes were both at the hospital, being treated for their injuries.

And Luke. Clarissa's gaze sought and found him beyond the chaos of the police station. Luke was safe. And so was she.

She hiked up her dress so she could walk without stepping on the hem and strode toward the captain's office where Luke waited on the bench outside the door. When she reached the bench, she collapsed next to him.

"How ya holding up, Luke?"

He stared straight ahead. "I'm a little numb."

She knew the feeling. Fully aware of what he was probably thinking, she slid her arm around his and leaned close. "Thanks for trying to help."

His gaze collided with hers, his brow furrowed

in confusion and irritation. "I almost got you killed. I brought the enemy right to you."

"And if you hadn't showed up when you did, I would be dead right now. You and Bainbridge were the distraction I needed to formulate an alternate plan of escape."

His frown relaxed. "I did?"

"That's right," she confirmed. "If you hadn't showed up when you did, I would be dead for sure." Pearson had heard enough of the conversation between her and Fuentes to send backup. But it was Luke's move and the cheerleaders who had bought her the time and opportunity she needed.

Luke sagged against the wall. "So I guess this is it." He turned his head to meet her eyes again. "I guess our marriage is over."

She had to smile. "Actually—" Clarissa leaned in close to whisper in his ear "—I was hoping we could get a new room, since yours is a crime scene, and have that encore you promised."

He smiled, the beauty of it taking her breath away. "You mean you're free to go?" He glanced around the crowded station. "You don't have to do a final report or anything?"

The bet she'd made with Kim and Dorian clearly included turning in the final report. "That can wait," she assured him. "But this—" she pressed a kiss to his handsome jaw "— can't."

Funny, Clarissa considered, as they left the station, she hadn't been looking for forever…and somehow she was pretty damned sure she had found it.

To Trudy Bulat—the coolest aunt I ever could have wished for. I'm so grateful to have married your nephew so he could share your awesome-ness with me! Thanks for all the support you've shown for my stories, even long before they ever saw print. I love you!

THE JOKER
Catherine Mann

CHAPTER ONE

BEING A PRINCESS was a real pain in the tiara.

Wearing the crown and fifty-plus-pound royal garb of her native country of Cantou threatened to give Las Vegas Police Detective Kim Wong a debilitating rash and backache. And the police station hadn't even been called to order for morning brief yet.

She shuffled from foot to foot, shoes too tight as she stood with her fellow police officers on the Las Vegas police force. Yeah, they were smirking.

"Zip it, Jakowski," Kim said, "or I'm gonna send your wife a picture of you in drag there."

Coughing into his hand, the smirker hushed and rejoined his conversation with an older detective in plaid shorts, a Hawaiian shirt and a camera around his neck.

Aside from this whole costume party being the strangest morning brief in history, the clothes brought back all the reasons she'd decided to put the pomp and circumstance behind her for a life where she controlled her choices. Hanging out with the coffeemaker burping sludge into the pot, Kim bolstered herself with thoughts of the wager she'd made with her two best pals, also detectives, Dorian Byrne and Clarissa Rivers.

The bet? Who would close their case first this weekend. The stakes? A very precious—and rare—week off. With staffing cuts, it was tough enough to snag a three-day weekend, much less a full week off. Except in a quirk of fate they had all qualified for the lone week off available—now it was a draw as to which of them could take it.

Their boss, Captain Bill Pearson, was riding the whole department's back to clean up the town the weekend before a big influx of tourists for the Labor Day extended holiday. Finishing up fast and first would rate extra kudos around the water cooler.

Every cop not on another detail had been assigned to work undercover in a suspect casino. She would be working the Great Wall Casino. The tip on the Great Wall would barely warrant attention on a normal day, but her boss was really wigging. So he was paying more attention than normal to an unreliable snitch with a heroin habit who vowed stolen diamonds were going to be moved through the Asian-themed casino this weekend, jewels somehow linked to a radical revolutionary group in Cantou.

Normally, they would just do a cursory check, not a deep undercover gig. Except this wasn't a normal weekend. Captain Pearson was definitely not in a normal mood, with politicians breathing down his neck and his wife breathing fire not too privately about all her husband's overtime.

So here Kim stood in fifty pounds of embroidered garb.

She raked her fingernails along her shoulder and resisted the urge to replace her tiara with a jeweled baseball cap. She truly respected the beauty and history of her heritage, but she'd picked a new path for her life years ago. However, for this weekend she had to impersonate her spoiled brat princess cousin, Ting.

Lucky for Kim's case, she and "Princess" Ting could be identical twins.

Not that either of them was really royalty. The whole imperial thing had ended thirty-eight years ago in a military coup. Her family was allowed to keep their titles out of courtesy only.

A hand rested on her shoulder, jolting her. She turned to find Dorian had slid through the masses, past a lion tamer and a vacationing couple. Dorian wore a prim suit, lucky her, but her undercover get-up would come soon enough.

"Hang in there, my friend," Dorian consoled. "It doesn't matter what you're wearing. We all know you can kick any man's ass with your black-belt qualifications—not to mention your street moxy."

Kim rolled her eyes. "I can barely walk in this thing. But sure, whatever."

Dorian dipped her head and whispered, "Kim, are you sure you're up to this?"

"I only needed a few stitches, not major surgery." Itching. Not pain. She wouldn't think about the bullet wound. A nick only, really.

"That doesn't mean getting shot didn't mess with your head."

Kim forced a smile. "You just want to shift the odds in your favor of getting that week off."

"I'm only watching my friend's back." She grinned. "Not that I could recognize your back in all those clothes you're wearing."

"It's better than being darn near naked," Kim pointed out—Dorian would be wearing street-walker gear soon enough.

A scowl turned Dorian's expression fierce. "Point taken. The stilettos are guaranteed ankle-breakers"

"I respect my country's historical wear, but dang, this stuff chafes."

"Once you get through the welcome ceremony at the Great Wall Casino, things will be more laid-back. You'll have freedom to dig around for leads on the diamond trafficking. Lucky for us, your family connections presented the perfect in. You should be able to move around without too much notice."

"Obviously you've never seen Ting featured in *Celebs Magazine*."

Clarissa Rivers made her way past Jakowski in drag to join them. "Too bad they couldn't give you a purple tiara. You like purple."

"I'm sure Ting has one shoved somewhere." Her cousin made full use of the family coffers to pamper herself.

"At least you don't have to go undercover as a maid or a hooker." Clarissa tugged at her outfit's apron in obvious disgust, the magenta costume obviously striking some kind of negative chord.

"You've got me there." Kim eyed her two friends, grateful for their support. They really could be out working their cases now, getting a head start on her, but they'd come here to look out for her, to make sure she had her feet under her since the shooting a month ago. "Thanks for coming over to check on me. But I'm sure you need to get back to your own assignments."

Clarissa tapped Kim's tiara. "We wouldn't have missed your launch for the world."

The room was called to attention for Captain Pearson. "Be seated. We've got a lot of ground to cover today, so let's get straight to it and start with getting Detective Wong out on the street."

Deep breath. Time to make her grand march to the front of the room. Bye-bye burping coffeepot.

Kim tossed her head back and strode forward, willing the crowd to part.

Which it did.

Hmm. Apparently the royal blood still shooshed through her veins after all. Her protective entourage—police officers all decked out in dark suits—flanked her on her way to the front of the room.

Captain Pearson nodded to her as he stepped aside to make room for Kim and company. "Good. You all look good, convincing. Well done, detectives. We'll get started soon. We're just waiting on one final individual, your personal bodyguard."

What? All itchy sensations disappeared in light of a full tingle of irritation. "Personal bodyguard? I think I'm insulted."

Pearson shook his head. "A bodyguard posing

as your escort. It will look strange in the casino if you don't have an escort."

"Of course, you're right." Irritation slid away, which then gave the itching full rein to return. "I'm thinking with my ego rather than my brain." She was still stinging after getting winged on that domestic dispute job last month. She didn't doubt herself, but she feared others would.

"We're concerned about security on this one, Wong. It goes beyond the jewels. There's been a threat called in on the royal family given the shaky relations between some rogue factions in the U.S. and in Cantou."

"I'm a U.S. citizen now."

"But you're not yourself this weekend."

Of course. Already her brain was getting muddled.

"This weekend, you are Ting in the eyes of your mother country. If the tip about a diamond transfer to fund underground armies in Cantou is true, they won't care if you're the princess or not. You're royal. That's cause enough to put a price on your head. So, regardless, we want a robust security detail, and what makes the most sense is a big burly boyfriend."

A boyfriend? She searched the room full of her fellow detectives. At least she could be sure she wasn't getting the jerk Jakowski, since he wouldn't scare off anybody in his spandex skirt and pink lipstick. Somebody really should have told him to shave his hairy legs.

Shuddering, she turned back to her boss. "You're kidding, sir."

"I'm afraid not," the captain said from behind the podium. "And the most logical choice would be the man well known for hanging out with the Wong women—"

A slight inkling started to niggle through. Oh, no.

"—when he was deployed to Cantou—"

He couldn't mean—

"—two years ago on assignment with the U.S. Air Force."

Oh, no. Pearson totally did mean—

The door opened wide and in lumbered Kim's bodyguard/escort to the whooping and applause of her fellow police officers, who must not have realized this man wore the uniform for real. He wasn't a rent-a-hunk.

Uh-uh. He was a man she wouldn't have forgotten regardless of his size. The looming guy wore Air Force blues, with a uniform jacket covered with ribbons and silver wings attesting to his career bravery. A military pilot who'd darn near stomped her heart a couple of years ago when she'd made her annual journey to her homeland. It should have been a fling. Instead, it had been an emotional code red, courtesy of the most intense, serious…sexy man she'd ever known.

Captain Marcus "Joker" Cardenas.

A HALF HOUR LATER as he marched down the dingy halls of the police station on his way to the limo with Kim, Marc figured he would do anything for his country. After all, he had served in uniform for ten years, fought overseas in the Middle East and Asia. He'd even lost a fiancée because of his devotion to the Air Force.

Yes, he would do anything for the USA. But acting as Kim Wong's bodyguard for a weekend was really pushing the envelope.

Still, Uncle Sam called for him to participate in this bizarre assignment for his country…. He hadn't even had a chance to say more than hello to the woman once he'd walked into the briefing room. Her boss had taken over and hadn't stopped talking until he dismissed them.

Two years ago Kim had gotten to him in a way no other woman had—and then dumped him on his patriotic butt. Her family, her country were all more important than him. And here they were again, except he didn't know if she'd changed.

What poor luck he'd been selected for this assignment—protecting a princess, even if she was pretending. Okay, not poor luck at all. He'd been on the short list of military contenders for the assignment. He'd been a military cop before entering flight training, and he'd worked some dark ops before. Plus the fact that he knew the woman and he became the perfect person to add to the protective detail.

But he *was* the best man for the job, and the thought of her in the line of fire twisted knots in his gut even now.

Damn. He could use some of that coffee they'd left behind.

What he didn't understand was if Kim Wong was a cop, a naturalized American, why had she been so tied to her country when they'd dated two years ago? It didn't make much sense to him.

Must have been a convenient brush-off.

Great. That made this assignment all the more fun. As if he wasn't already pretty much mad at the world. Shortly after he and Kim had split, he'd fallen into a rebound relationship with a woman who lived near his base. She'd been the opposite of adventurous Kim. Seemed perfect for settling down.

Wrong.

His fiancée had dumped him at the rehearsal dinner a year ago because of his dangerous job. Fine. So he'd taken some shrapnel when his barracks had been blown to bits. It wasn't like his job had been a surprise to her. If he heard one more friend say how it was better he found out now, he would knock their block off.

Yeah, yeah, he wasn't an easygoing, chuckle-a-minute sort of fellow, but it took a lot to make him mad, too. For the most part he was unshakable.

Pity pissed him off. So what would Kim think of the scar he sported on his face now? And was that even Kim under all that red-and-orange embroidered garb? It was wrapped so tightly around her he wasn't sure she would be able to make her way to the limo waiting outside.

The crowd stalled in the hall near the exit sign, apparently some holdup with traffic outside. The two women flanking Kim thrust out their hands.

"Morning, Captain Cardenas," said an uptight chick in a suit buttoned so snugly it might well choke her. "Dorian Byrne."

"Nice to meet you." He went through the motions, his eyes still on Kim.

"And good morning to you." The lady in a rosy-red maid's costume started to shake his hand before pausing to scratch her arm.

Poison ivy, or what? Nothing contagious, he hoped. He shook her hand and prayed for the best. "I assume you're detectives who work with Kim."

Detective Uptight pursed her lips so flat even a collagen implant wouldn't have survived. "Yes, sir, we do. And I assume you've got some exceptional training for them to have brought you in, because Kim's never needed backup to this degree before."

The cop/maid waved a finger in his face. "There's some serious crap going down at the Great Wall this weekend."

Kim snorted. "Yeah, right, heavy crap, Scooter says. Which doesn't mean much from a heroin-addicted snitch who likes to think he's a real cop because he manages to hold down a job guarding furniture storage containers."

Still, even with Kim's dismissive comment, the warnings of danger at the Great Wall Casino sent a shot of premonition up his spine he hadn't felt since seconds before his barracks blew underneath him over in Rubistan. He was supposed to be her body-guard, but he'd been told this was a low-key gig. The thought of something actually going down… The 9mm strapped to his waist under his uniform jacket brought him much-needed reassurance. He would use any means at hand to keep her safe.

Kim perched a hand on her hip. "Thanks, pals, but I *am* here and can talk for myself. I am smart enough to take whatever help they give me—as long as that help is smart enough not to get under my feet so much we are tripping over each other."

A not-so-subtle reference to the way they'd met, slamming into each other in an open-air market. Her hands full of fruit. His arms full of kimonos and pearls to give his family—suddenly smashed with all her produce.

They'd both laughed so hard he couldn't help but be entranced by her smile, the crinkle in the corner of her eyes. The fact was that very few people made him smile. He came by his call sign Joker as a joke in itself, because he was renowned for having no sense of humor. Somehow around Kim, the world seemed…lighter.

Or it had then. Not so much now. Not with a breakup between them and jewel thieves near the deposed princess of Cantou, Ting Wong or Wong Ting. He never could get the name order right in the traditions of her world but he'd tried.

She'd tried.

They'd failed.

And it hurt.

With the broken engagement dogging his ass as

well as his screwed up relationship with Kim, he wasn't in the mood for anything serious.

"Uh, are you still with us?" Rosy Clothes Maid interrupted his thoughts. "We really just stopped by to give you a send-off, but if you two are going to stand here and do some kind of Bogey and Bergman moony-eyed thing, I'm going to punch out now and let you finish on your own timetable." She hitched a thumb over her shoulder at Detective Uptight. "Besides, Dorian's got a date with a garter belt and merry widow."

Now that snagged his attention, except such clothing was in his mind on a different female…. Kim.

He stared into her eyes, all he could do with this hall full of people around them. Probably for the best since their last meeting had been a roaring argument, so unlike him. So very like the tumultuous woman who'd spun his world more than any barrel roll in an airplane.

A shrill whistle split the air, along with a shout to head out. The road was cleared.

"Well, Kim, it looks like we're about ready to load up, so I guess from here on out I'm supposed to call you Ting."

She flinched. "Yes, I imagine so. I've thought through the whole undercover op and hadn't con-

sidered that one part—the name change. Ting."
She smiled that secret smile of hers that used to
bring him to her or her to him and lead to…

No. Stop. This was to be a protective detail and
some downtime in a casino. Nothing more.

Then she smiled again and he knew it could be
far more if they weren't careful. She glanced over
her shoulder as if gauging the privacy level,
stepped closer to him and lowered her voice.
"Marc, for what it's worth, I am sorry about the
way things ended. We both deserved a better
farewell than a public argument. And speaking of
public, that's probably all we need to say here."

Part of him wanted to trust she meant what she
said, because then he could close the door on a relationship that had tainted his broken engagement
of a year ago. But that same broken engagement
also made him leery of trusting anyone right now,
especially his own instincts when it came to
women. Kim—Ting—could very well be offering
up this reconciliation as a part of her job, to help
make their fake relationship look all the more
real. That tiny seed of doubt took hefty root in his
mind.

Either way—truth or playing a game—his
answer would be the same. He smiled right back,
ready to press on out that exit door and into the

waiting limo. "Then I guess lady luck has shined on us after all, because we've been given a second chance to say goodbye with less fanfare this go round."

CHAPTER TWO

KIM DECIDED SHE MUST be a freak, because sitting in the backseat of a luxurious limo with tinted windows gave her a serious case of the heebie-jeebies.

Okay, technically "flashback" would be the correct term, according to the shrink the police department had made her see after the shootout. A shootout that had nicked her and killed her partner.

She'd spent more time than she liked on "Dr. Freud's" couch, discussing her smothering childhood limousine days when she'd had no life of her own, every move dictated by her royal grandparents. Her parents and Ting's had both died before Kim's teens in a fluke skiing accident—an avalanche. Her grandmother had been terrified of losing the remaining members of her family and determined the two girls would do the old ways proud.

Breaking away seven years ago had been hard, really hard, especially since she did love her family. But she wanted a life free of the money, extravagance and trappings, as much as her cousin Ting embraced the whole kit and caboodle.

And the part that still bit most? Meeting Marc… Knowing Marc… Giving up Marc because of family pressure two years ago had been the spurring event that had given her the backbone to make the break permanent. Of course he'd let her go mighty easily, stinging her pride, sealing her decision. Up until then, she'd simply played at being a cop. Running home every time her grandmother called for her to participate in some special function.

After Marc, she found the guts to tell her family no more sprinting home at their whim—and she put in her papers to be considered for detective.

Now he sat beside her again, his hot leg muscles pressed to hers. How she could feel him through the layers of clothing and beading, she had no idea, but his heat, his touch…

Oh, yes. She felt it.

She shifted her attention away from him and to the window, most of Las Vegas apparently still sleeping off their partying from the night before. Light tourist traffic meandered along the sidewalks—casinos and showplaces oddly dimmer during the day with at least a few of their thousands of lights off.

Kim's fingers traced over the swirling patterns stitched into the fiery, heavy brocade enclosing her like a swaddling blanket. The cars with her entourage streamed ahead and behind, just as suffocating as ever. She enjoyed her freedom from the strictures of her position at home and when she missed seeing everyone, she now made an annual trip to Cantou to say "howdy."

Yet, after she had the chitchat with the department shrink, she realized that sometimes she subconsciously held on to old habits—like how she always picked big, four-wheel drives when car shopping. She needed that sense of metal around her—without the all-service bar and cable television. Hell, there had been three assassination attempts made on her life before she was ten.

Had those early attempts on her life left a mark that made this recent shooting take a heavier toll on her than normal? What was a normal reaction for being shot at? For having her partner gunned down?

She shook off the memory and focused on the present. The part about how being chauffeured didn't set well with her. While they skimmed past fountains and palm trees, she wanted to tap the little conversation window and ask the two undercover cops up front if they'd gotten the final score on last night's Dodgers game. She'd been too itchy and had taken a late-night run. How odd that her job had brought her full circle back to the old days.

To Marc. His hot, muscular thigh.

And his scowling square jaw—with an unexplained new scar.

Whoever thought up the call sign Joker for this pensive pilot sure had a twisted sense of humor.

Might as well talk now while she knew they weren't being listened to. No bugs in the limo. "Have you ever been to Vegas before?"

His somber expression didn't change other than the slight upward quirk of one brow. "Do you or do you not remember anything we said to each other?"

Duh. She wanted to thunk herself on the forehead. "Oh, right, your flag exercises you told me about."

"Red Flag and Green Flag—" slowly he nodded yet he seemed to be watching elsewhere even as he spoke to her "—would be a couple of annual exercises, yes."

"Practice war."

"Exactly."

"Like the times you've battled in Cantou." Where did that semicombative comment come from? How simplistic those few words made such a convoluted political situation sound.

Truly, she'd never thought of him as the enemy

in any way. Could she be trying to put emotional distance between them to make up for the physical closeness they would be forced to endure over the next couple of days?

"Anything is a possibility these days, but we're hopeful for more stability in the region."

She'd been reassured the car wasn't bugged, but even if it was, nothing they said contained any State secrets. Could she trust Scooter's tip about the diamonds passing through the casino this weekend? Cantou certainly enjoyed more peace these days, but there were still factions that wanted things to return to the old ways.

Actually, that wasn't totally true. They didn't want a benevolent ruler. They wanted a dictatorship. Nothing she'd seen in the intel on these rebel factions showed anything benevolent. Of course, every country had its radicals....

She shuddered at the satellite images of extensive torture. Burial sites later found.

No. If these jewels truly did exist, they would not make it into the hands of those monsters to finance their revolution. The stones, the opportunity for such massive capital, would stop with her. She would find their courier in the Great Wall.

Marc took her cold hand in his.

She jerked as if electrified.

"What?" he said. "We're a couple. We should get used to touching each other again."

Okay, two could play this game—and he *was* right. She pulled a tighter smile and linked her fingers with his.

Marc winked, the levity so strange on such a grim face. "Now, that's my girl."

Girl? "Excuse me, but I haven't been a 'girl' in quite a few years."

"Pardon me, then." His leg pressed harder, his arm sliding along the back of the seat—along her shoulders. "Woman. Lady. One hot babe. Take your pick."

Awareness seared through her until it was all she could do to hold still because moving would give away how much he still affected her.

Maybe silence would work best after all.

She swallowed back any words, along with a crazy, stupid image of what it would be like to kiss him quiet. Not the kind of silence that seemed wise at the moment. Still her gaze held his dark eyes for what must have been at least two traffic lights, and then he broke contact, frowning even deeper, if that was possible.

The car jerked, slamming her against him.

"What the—" she yelled, looking forward to the drivers.

"Down!" Marc shouted, palming her back and pushing her toward the floorboards. "Guns! Outside."

Pop, pop, pop cut through the air. A dark blue Mercedes roared beside them. The nose of a gun peeked from the window but no faces—all seen in a blur of peripheral perception on their way to the floor.

The limo swerved again. Harder. Marc? Was he okay? She didn't have time to check, only protect. Except he had a gun in his hand that he'd gotten from heaven only knew where.

Horns honked. Skidding tires squealed as someone outside screamed. What had happened to the cars following and leading them? Her entourage?

Heart racing, she braced a hand against the door, reaching under her skirt for the gun strapped to her leg to fire back. Peeking up, she took aim through the broken window....

The Mercedes raced ahead. Away. Disappearing around a corner as quickly as it had slid beside them.

"Marc? Marc?" She turned to check on him and found him launching toward the front seat, obviously in solid health.

Then she noticed her driver, the undercover cop in front. The unconscious, possibly dead Vincent slumped over the wheel, his foot resting on the gas. Damn it, why couldn't he have slouched on the brake? His partner, Tim, hung limp against his shoulder harness. Both men dripped blood.

No wonder the car swerved so horribly. They were so screwed.

Marc continued to try to wedge through the communication window, but his shoulders were too broad for him to fit through.

"Move!" Kim shouted.

"Right." Backing out of the window, he grabbed her by the waist and shoved her through. Her costume stuck halfway.

"Damn it!" She reached and grabbed for the steering wheel as the car careened toward running pedestrians. A new bride ran across the street with her groom wearing Elvis sequins.

Kim hammered the horn. Hard. Again and again, and yes! The people on the street and the other cars listened and got the hell out of the way, into other lanes or onto a sidewalk. Not that she could even hear the horn. Adrenaline sang in her ears, threatening to drown out anything Marc might have said, as the sides of the window bit into her hips while she hung suspended over the driver's seat.

The limo still swerved, going forty-five miles per hour. They were safe for the moment, until

Marc could wedge her through and into the front seat where she could reach the pedals. Thank heaven for the lack of traffic or they would all be taking the eternal dirt nap.

Marc ripped the bulkier part of the costume from around her waist, while she swerved the limo around obstacles. With inches to spare, she avoided an ATM on the corner, then just missed a light pole on the next corner. Finally, air swished over her legs. She didn't have time for modesty. Only relief.

She felt Marc's hand planted firmly on her satin-and-lace-underwear-clad butt a second before he shoved. And what a weird time to try to remember what kind of underwear she'd put on this morning. It so shouldn't matter because they could die, but if she had to die, she didn't want her last moments to be with her showing a man boring undies.

Then she remembered…orange lace.

Oh, my.

Totally see-through orange lace.

Oof. She landed in a tangled heap on top of unconscious Vincent. Possibly dead Vincent, and didn't that sober her thoughts up right away? She couldn't think of him now or even risk a glance at Tim, not with the car swerving, bumping off the curb.

Finally she wedged herself in Vincent's lap. Ugh. It was the only way to get to the wheel. Gasping for air and a steadier heart rate, she kicked his foot off the gas pedal and inched hers over the brake.

So why had they lurched ahead?

"Damn," Marc shouted from the back. "We've got another problem."

Kim wrestled with the wheel while a new car behind rammed them. She worked to stay on the road, veering away from the young mother pushing a double stroller, keeping the car under control not as easy as it seemed during the police academy. "What's going on now?"

"That bump wasn't random," Marc answered. "We're being followed. And by followed, I mean bumper to bumper, they want us off the road."

The limo surged forward again. Her mind raced. Where was the nearest police station? If she could get there, a place of law enforcement, their pursuers would leave.

Marc reached through the conversation window and stripped the weapons from the wounded— possibly dead—men up front. "If you have another gun tucked away somewhere, hand it over so I can deal with our problem in back. Meanwhile, just drive."

CHAPTER THREE

JUST DRIVE? THE WORDS ricocheted around in Kim's head harder than the force of the SUV that had almost catapulted their limousine into the next county.

So just drive? Easier said than done. This vehicle was a freaking tank to handle. She'd never driven anything remotely like it before.

Kim gripped the limo's wheel tighter in a white-knuckled grip while Marc gathered up his arsenal of weapons off the two shot and bleeding men beside her in the front seat.

"Careful," she shouted over her shoulder.

"I know," he hollered back. "There are pedestrians everywhere."

As if on cue, an elderly couple jumped back from the curb onto the sidewalk, clutching each other while his camera clunked against her touristy tote bag. Kim hoped she hadn't given them heart failure for what was probably their fiftieth wedding anniversary trip. Talk about making a memory.

Marc angled out the window and popped off a shot at the looming SUV behind them, ducking back in a second before another bump that would have sent him flying. She checked the rearview mirror. The SUV still trailed them, but in the other lane for the moment at least.

And damned if the old man back on the sidewalk hadn't started snapping pictures while his wife jotted notes on a piece of paper. License plate numbers, hopefully. Chalk one up for the citizen's watch gang.

Kim yanked her attention back to the road. She slid one hand from the wheel and grabbed the police radio from Vincent's waist. "Marc, can you take this, please, and call the station. Tell them to put out an alert to the cops in the area. It's just three blocks up, I believe. Ask them to be waiting. That should get rid of our friends."

Marc's hand thrust through the window. "Good thinking."

He snagged the radio in a flash and she heard his voice making the call while she swerved from lane to lane.

"All set," he called from the back, his voice steady, reassuring. "They're putting calls to all cars. But with your driving and this firepower, sweetheart, I could hold them off in my sleep."

Too bad they were both very much awake during this nightmare.

KIM HADN'T EXPECTED TO SEE the police station's coffee sludge again today. Except the pot wasn't full now. Just sporting an inch left for whatever brave soul dared pour the remaining dregs into one of the cups stacked beside the dairy creamer.

Kim stared at the coffeepot, her morning scrolling through her mind while Marc loomed, brooding. She'd been shot at by a gunman, rammed by a maniac in a Mercedes and had survived a mad dash to a police station with her limo sporting a flat tire.

Hmm... Even she didn't dare risk the remains of that coffeepot.

She turned her back to the counter. Of course, Captain Pearson's angry face as he stalked into the briefing room for the second time today was darn near as frightening as the java pot behind her.

"What the hell happened out there, Wong?"

"We're fine, sir, thanks for asking," Kim couldn't resist quipping. It would have been polite if he'd said something nice about being glad she was still alive, for Pete's sake. "Sir, I believe I summed it up fairly extensively when I called on the way over here."

"This is not good, Wong. Not good at all."

She scratched at the raw spot on her shoulder even though she wore a pair of Las Vegas Metropolitan Police Department sweatpants and a T-shirt, since her once-gorgeous costume was ruined. "Sir, I'm far from pleased myself at the turn of events, but at least Vincent and Tim are alive."

For now. Vincent was still in surgery. Tim couldn't remember anything, the bullet grazing his head having apparently messed with his memory.

"I've got cops in the hospital, a shot-up limo and Scooter the snitch found dead of an overdose behind the Great Wall Casino."

The blood in her veins iced. Stakes rose by the second as that so-called unreliable tip grew exponentially in importance. She had Marc to think about, as well. Sure, he had his own credentials, but she preferred to work with people who didn't stir a wash of unsettling feelings she couldn't afford to examine right now.

Pearson scrubbed a hand over his sweating bald head. "We're going to give this another shot."

"Shot." She winced. "Not my favorite word today, sir."

"Fair enough." He passed her a large brown box. A box around fifty pounds… "First off, you need to get outfitted again."

Yeah, fifty pounds. That would be about right. She sighed, the raw patches of skin aching already. Marc continued to loom and silently brood while Pearson paced and spelled out their adjusted plan.

"You can make your grand appearance right before the evening banquet rather than the afternoon musical show as originally planned. That gives us time to regroup and clear a safe route. We'll need more protective detail than originally slated, especially for that costume ball on Saturday."

He shook his head.

In all the hoopla the reality of this hadn't hit her until now. Someone had tried to kill her—or rather kill a Cantou princess. Scooter was dead.

The tip about the underground dealings, rebel factions of dictatorship hopefuls and a passel of jewels was real. Beyond her job, she had a duty to her country and her family to stop these criminals.

The box in her hands just got a lot heavier.

THE PAGEANTRY DARN NEAR smothered her once again as they unloaded in front of the Great Wall Casino. At least they'd made it here in one piece this time.

Still, Kim longed for tickets to a Dodgers game or a picnic in the park with her dog and a friend.

Marc, perhaps?

She'd never had the chance to show him the world she preferred, although she'd told him about it. Why then had she choked at coming back to the U.S. with him just because of family pressure? She was here now. If they'd met this weekend, things might have been different.

Except she would have wanted to meet the man he was then, the one who smiled. Sure, he'd never been a laugh-a-minute sort, but he'd had a half smile and slight crinkle to the corner of his eyes…. He'd been a one-liner funny guy, rather than this somber fellow who never spoke.

Hooking her hand in the crook of Marc's elbow, Kim made her way up the red carpeted stairs slowly, the narrow skirt constricting her steps. "People are not going to believe we're a couple if you keep glaring at me like that. Although I guess you're glaring at everyone."

"I have reason to be concerned," he whispered in a low growl while still cupping his hand over hers in a warm caress that made her stumble. "Someone tried to kill you today and that pisses me off."

"Oh." She regained her footing and focused on making her way toward the gilded doors.

He was upset for her? That shaded things differently, regardless of how much she wanted to deny the feelings zinging through her. Why had she run from him before?

Oh yeah. Loss of her independence to such a strong personality. Reluctance to totally cut ties with her country.

Scared of losing more people she loved.

She could almost hear Ting cackling with laughter and mocking her for being a chicken. Kim shushed the Ting voice and asserted herself. "I *am* able to defend myself, Marc. I'm a trained police officer."

"I realize that," he acknowledged with a slight nod. "It doesn't change a thing for me."

"Well, you need to change the glare before we walk through the doors or people will wonder why I haven't given you the boot."

"Fair enough." He turned toward her and his eyes heated over her with such desire she downright shivered.

Fake, she reminded herself. He was pretending. She had to keep herself grounded in the reality that this was an undercover op, but darn, it was tough.

She swallowed hard. "Good. That's, uh, exactly right. Now we can walk inside."

Two bellmen pushed the doors open, the swell

of voices and a gong welcoming her. Head back with a gestalt she'd been taught from the cradle, she entered.

The environment of the casino enveloped her. The sounds—bells, whistles and chimes from the machines. People—laughing, groaning, cheering and calling bets. The bustle. Smells of the buffet across the way, while drinks closer by flowed freely. The place was more than a little hokey in its Great Wall theme, sometimes downright clichéd, but she had to confess, there were flashes and bits of the decor that made her nostalgic.

Who to trust? No one. She was royal today.

She clutched Marc's arm and pressed deeper inside. The mayhem of the Great Wall Casino quieted in a rippling wave as everyone slowly caught on to look toward the entranceway.

One of the beadings on her new costume jabbed her armpit, but now wouldn't be a particularly good time to reach inside and fix the annoying and increasingly painful problem. Tough it out and pray she didn't bleed to death from a lethal silver stud.

The casino owner shoved through the crowd toward her, wringing his hands. "Your Highness, Your Highness, we're honored to have you here this weekend at our humble establishment."

"Thank you, Mr. Chiang, we are most pleased to be here and look forward to enjoying a much-needed vacation from royal responsibilities." She turned to Marc. "Where would you like to start, sweetie?"

"Your assistant has the schedule. I'm just here to enjoy looking at you, Ting baby." He flashed that killer smile again.

Baby? She resisted the urge to roll her eyes.

Her assistant, Sun, an undercover cop who worked street patrol, scurried to the front with a PDA and stylus. "You have a photo op at the Fountain of Many Fortunes before you can change into more comfortable clothing."

Comfortable clothes. Magic words. Kim squeezed Marc's arm. "Then by all means, let us find that fountain."

Holy guacamole Marc had muscles under that uniform jacket. How had she forgotten the sturdy feel of him? A memory of those arms banded around her waist as she arched up to kiss him flashed through her mind at this most inopportune time. Then it hit her. She had a real problem that could prove to be a serious distraction this weekend.

It was so not cool having a hot bodyguard in uniform whose body she happened to want *out* of that uniform.

THE LAST OF THE FLASHBULBS popped and snapped, leaving Marc seeing stars and blinking hard. He didn't like the momentary blindness that left him vulnerable and unable to protect himself or Kim.

Not to mention the sparking-lights sensation it brought on that came mighty damn close to that of sitting in a cockpit, seeing tracers streak across the sky in front of his windscreen. He really hated how things snuck up on him that way—like Fourth of July fireworks. Big displays were okay, but the surprise firecrackers some neighbors set off…those left him flinching. The mind was a funky organ with a will of its own and a healing timetable Marc couldn't seem to facilitate. Just grit his teeth and move forward.

Palm flat on Kim's back, he led her through the throng, fountains gushing beside them in a multicolored display while a live band played in the background. Reporters swooped around them in a crush that made him nervous for security reasons.

A woman with a notepad pushed closer to Kim. "Are you and the pilot serious about each other?"

Kim smiled and snuggled closer. "What's serious?"

A microphone was shoved under Marc's nose

from some man in a bad suit. "Will you be living in America or will he ask for a transfer overseas?"

He growled low. "Premature question."

And older woman with a photographer at her side shouted, "Are there wedding bells in the future?"

The scar along his jaw itched. Wedding bells? Been there. Tried that. Lost the bride. "No comment."

An Ichabod Crane look-alike asked, "Will this strengthen ties between our countries?"

Marc pushed forward, cutting a swathe through with his arm. "Definitely no comment. We're on vacation."

Kim held up a regal hand and smiled benevolently. "It is far too early in our relationship to speculate. We simply want to enjoy ourselves, watch some shows, perhaps gamble a little."

"But wasn't he rumored to be dating a royal in your country two years ago? Was that you or your cousin?"

"Me, of course." She smiled possessively. "For a brief time. Now we're getting reacquainted. So your princess and the soldier fairy tale—while quite romantic, I must admit—is a bit hasty. If you give us the privacy to explore possible feelings, then we will be able to give the four of you an exclusive all the sooner."

Suggestive laugher rippled through, making Marc want to punch somebody's lights out. How had she put up with this kind of mayhem growing up? No wonder she'd shed it all.

Kim squealed beside him, yanking him back to the present and reminding him that while romance might be their cover, it couldn't play out for real. The distraction would prove too costly.

Someone's—Kim's—life.

He jerked, his every instinct going on high alert as he wrapped an arm around her waist and pulled her to him.

"What's wrong?" he whispered in her ear.

She stayed stiff against him, her eyes wide and…indignant? "That man over there," she said, pointing to her left, "he felt me up."

What the…? Marc followed her pointing finger to the back of a male in a waiter's uniform, pushing through the crowd so fast—disappearing. Not a chance they would find him, much less catch him, especially when they hadn't even seen his face.

Marc shifted his attention back to Kim and getting her away from the reporters and the crowd. She molded herself to his side as he hustled her toward the elevator pronto. No more of this hanging around for photo ops or questions. She'd been shot at and someone had broken through the protective circle all in a few short hours.

Enough.

They needed to get upstairs to the penthouse and regroup.

Once the elevator doors swished shut, he allowed himself to breathe. "Are you all right?"

She sagged back against one of the mirrored walls, feeling along her side as elevator music did little to soothe the tense atmosphere. "There's a hole in my clothes, right here along the seam."

"What?" He started to probe and then realized—gulp—she had on an orange satin-and-lace bra that matched those panties he'd seen up close and personal in the limo earlier.

Adrenaline may have been shooting through his veins in that life-or-death moment, but he would have had to be *dead* not to notice that luscious display of curves in hot lingerie. And now, here they were again. Alone. No gunmen or ramming cars. He cleared his throat, though he couldn't do much about his raging libido. She'd said something about a problem with a guy in the lobby. Marc forced his mind to focus on that, not the enticing curve of breast peeking through Kim's torn clothing.

"That creep didn't just feel me up. He tore off a piece of my clothing." Her indignation crackled off her like the lights sparking off the beading on her native costume.

"Deep breaths." And he kept his eyes locked on hers, yet somehow found those no less distracting than the curve of her breast. Damn. He was still a serious sap when it came to this woman. Right now, though, he needed to get her calmed down so they could both watch her back. Nothing came before her safety. "I know you're upset and you have every right. But you're okay."

The doors shooshed open to the penthouse level. He momentarily went on high alert again, his hand covering his weapon at his waist under his jacket…. But the hall gaped empty.

"I may not like how uncomfortable the ceremonial outfit is and I may have complained and been a brat about wearing this. But, damn it, this is the ceremonial garb of my mother country and that jerk defiled it. I do not take that lightly."

The regal tip of her chin caught him off guard. He was so used to seeing the woman who preferred jeans and ball caps. Even knowing she'd chosen her family ties over him, even seeing her date the man her grandmother had selected, still Marc saw her as *his* laid-back Kim.

But the woman who'd held on to her imperial

roots two years ago still existed, and Marc had the distinct impression that the royal was every bit as bad-ass tough as the cop standing before him silently fuming.

CHAPTER FOUR

CLOTHING UNPACKED AND CHANGED, Kim stood in front of the dressing room mirror, at least semire-laxed from the shower.

Okay. Not at all relaxed. At least she'd washed the perspiration from the stress of the day from her body and had a chance to let-down and shake for a few minutes without worrying about appearing brave.

Now she combed her hair, appreciating her new clothes—a sheath dress with a high neck, emerald green. It had the look of her country, as well, but was more contemporary. So she still played her role, but with less itch.

Marc sprawled in a chair over by the window in their luxurious accommodations, hand-painted fans decorating the walls. He watched. He waited. Other than during her shower, he hadn't let her out of his sight. He certainly made for an efficient bodyguard.

They had plenty of protection in their two-bedroom suite with the front sitting area full of the entourage of undercover cops. Still, Marc stayed. His eyes glued to her while he remained silent.

She shivered.

Maybe if they talked, or something, this would feel less intimate, the getting dressed together. "So tell me what you've been doing for the past two years."

"I'm still in the air force, stationed at Charleston Air Force Base in South Carolina."

Duh. "The uniform tipped me off."

And wow, did he ever look hot in his formal uniform—a mess dress, he'd called it, dark blue and full of shiny medals attesting to his bravery.

His reflection blinked slowly as she brushed snarls out of her damp hair. "I could have gotten out of the air force but still be wearing the uniform, you know."

"You're too young to retire," she said. He was thirty-two to her twenty-nine.

His gaze held hers for an unblinking minute. "There are medical retirements."

Her own recent near miss with a gunshot wound ached. "You were injured?"

She spun around, comb in hand, and made a quick sweep of the medals on his jacket hanging on the back of a chair and, oh my, yes, she saw a Purple Heart. Her heart pounded heavy and fast against her ribs. She'd somehow overlooked the Purple Heart in the rows of ribbons on his other uniform he'd worn 'earlier. The less formal uniform had so many more of the small rectangular ribbons it was easy to have missed the one indicating he'd been injured in the line of duty.

Now she couldn't miss the symbol of his wound, pain endured.

Having served with men on the police force, though, she knew more than a little about tiptoeing around the male ego, so she kept her voice low-key. "What happened to earn you that purple piece of bling there?"

He kept his casual sprawl in the wingback chair, backlit by the multicolored overload of lights of Las Vegas. As high up as they were, they didn't have to worry about gunmen through the window, so they didn't need to avoid the windows. She waited for his answer…suddenly realizing her palms hurt from the cut of her fingernails digging in from her tight fists.

She unfurled her fingers and rested them on his arm. "Marc?"

"Barracks bombing. I lived and walked away." Muscles bunched and jumped under her touch, the only sign of his tension. "Others weren't so lucky. We lost a crewmember. Another almost died in surgery."

"You were injured, though." Her hand rose of its own volition to stroke along his jaw, the ribbed tissue a new addition from when she'd known him before. "The scar here?"

He nodded.

She swallowed hard as she thought of what could have happened. "Much lower and it would have sliced your neck."

"The thought crossed my mind."

She understood that. She'd spent countless sleepless hours in her bed going over what-ifs of the shooting that had nicked her and cost her partner his life. "Were you hurt anywhere else?"

"You're mighty curious." He sat up straight for the first time, leaning forward. Closer. His freshly showered soapy scent caught her already raw senses unawares. "Are you one of those groupies?"

She stood her ground. "Did the war make you rude? You know me better than that."

"Sorry." He clapped a hand on his chest just shy of his heart. "I caught a shard of flying glass here, too."

Her own heart skipped a beat…and another. "You really did almost die." And she never would have known. Nobody would have told her. She had no contacts in his world. Their short romance had been during his leave time while he was deployed overseas.

Would she have felt the loss of his presence in the universe? Her grandmother had believed that the flow of ch'i connected spirit and consciousness on both the personal level and the global, and while Kim had turned her back on much of her old-world ways, in this…yes, she wanted to think she would have sensed it if a strong being like Marc had left this life.

She couldn't stop herself. Maybe it was leftover adrenaline from nearly being shot earlier, or the emotional rush of hearing his starkly told story now, but she had to touch him. Just to feel the vital heat of him and ground them both in this world.

Kim flattened her palm to his chest, over his heartbeat that had come so close to being stilled forever. "I'm glad you're all right."

"Me, too." His mouth tipped in one of those rare smiles of his, a real smile, not the fake kind that spread a bit broader.

She couldn't stop the words from spilling from her mouth. "It's still tough walking away when someone else didn't."

His fathomless brown eyes widened in surprise. "You know."

"I do." Her knees went wobbly and before she knew it, he'd caught her between his knees. Oh my. His hand palmed her back to steady her.

He cupped the back of her head and pulled her to his chest, his chin resting on her damp hair for a long, heated sigh as if he'd been waiting for this moment.

Slowly, her body came to life in his embrace. The hard cut of biceps encircled her. The broad stretch of bulging pecs pressed against her, reminding her she stood a full eight inches shorter than he did. Oh, the feel of standing between his legs... They hadn't made love before, but they'd come close. So close, she'd regretted missing out on the experience more than once over the years.

Her toes curled in the carpet. She wasn't the type for casual sex, but how she wanted him right now.

Adrenaline, she reminded herself. Life and death and a Purple Heart. She needed to get her head on straight again.

Kim backed away with more than a little regret, but enough wobbly resolve to put at least a couple of inches between her and the only man ever to live in her thoughts beyond the break-up. "My hair is going to leave a wet spot on your fancy shirt. We should both finish getting dressed for supper."

"Of course, but I'll be within shouting distance if the least little thing seems off. Do you understand? Anything. Call me." Standing, he kept the safe couple of inches between them, his hand still curved around the back of her neck, cradling the sensitive nape. "And, Kim?"

"Yes?"

"Thank you." He dipped his head and brushed his mouth over hers so gently, so quickly, she could have persuaded herself she imagined the whole kiss—if the touch hadn't set her nerves tingling.

By the time she'd shaken off the tingles and come back to the present, she watched the door to his room click closed behind him. Now that he'd taken his tempting self elsewhere, only the lingering scent of his cologne left behind, her brain hitched on a mystery she should have discerned right away.

Thank you for what?

TWO HOURS LATER seated at the head dinner table, Marc reached over his egg drop soup for the pepper mill. He didn't like how they all sat on pillows on the floor, feeling distinctly at a disadvantage if someone launched an attack. However, what could he do?

To make matters worse, Kim's words still echoed in his ears as she sat to his right on her cushion. She'd rocked him more with a single sentence than his ex-fiancée had the entire time they were engaged.

How had she known what it felt like to survive when even his friends hadn't? Certainly his fiancée hadn't. Could it be Kim had a point of reference from her past in Cantou as well as assassination attempts that took people who worked for her family?

He'd considered questioning her on the subject earlier, even had the words formed and ready to spill out, but stopped. Such a discussion would only serve to deepen the level of intimacy that had already been heating out of control fast enough on its own. Much more closeness and they may not have made it down to supper.

Marc finished off his soup and a second egg roll. He couldn't help but think of his return from overseas and how Carol had never once said, "I'm glad you're alive." Instead, she'd focused on, "I can't stand this way of life."

Sure, he understood. It would be hell to live not

knowing if the person you loved—or claimed to love—would be coming home or not. But damn, he'd expected something in the way of a tearful "Welcome home." Like Kim's straightforward sentence and head resting on his chest.

This simple assignment wasn't turning out to be so simple after all.

He fiddled with his cuff links, his cummerbund and bowtie confining but necessary. He preferred his flight suit and black leather boots, but what could he do? This was the job before him.

And yeah, he wondered if he'd nudged his way into this job because somehow unresolved business with Kim had caused him to sabotage his engagement a year ago. No woman seemed to measure up to the lady seated next to him.

Damn, he hated thinking about his broken engagement at all, much less now when he had another relationship screwup on the mind. Must be the uniform. He hadn't had the thing out since the night before his wedding, when his ex-fiancée had decided she didn't want to be married to a military man and always wonder if he would come home alive or not.

He vaguely noted the soup being taken away and replaced by the main course of peanut chicken. He clicked his chopsticks together absently while he waited for Kim to be served first.

He was tired of hearing how it was better to have found out before the wedding. People might be right—they *were* right—but hearing it over and over again didn't make him feel one damn bit better.

People didn't like their faces rubbed in "right." So why did they feel compelled to keep on doing it to others? One of life's great mysteries, right up there with Stonehenge and why a man lost the ability to think rationally when he saw a flash of woman's lingerie?

Yet he couldn't escape the disconcerting fact that Kim, fully clothed in a dress subtly hugging her gentle curves, unsettled him just as much as Kim showing hints of her sexy underwear.

Hell, dude, he reminded himself. *Be respectful.*

Sure, he needed to act the boyfriend role, not like some over-revved lech. He dragged his gaze back up to her face.

Her frowning face. Furrows dug deep trenches in her forehead, shadows cast by the low lantern lights—that dim lighting being another security risk that irked him.

She leaned close to him, her shoulder touching his as she brought her mouth up to his ear. "Ting is allergic to peanuts."

Protective instincts went on high alert as he glanced at the peanut chicken. His arm shot along the back of her shoulders. He cupped her closer to him, scanning the room. "Your assistant would have let them know, right?"

"Absolutely. It's part of the planning package that's sent ahead before a royal goes anywhere," she said as if it should be basic knowledge, except that would be commonplace in her world.

Now all the food on the table seemed suspect. No wonder kings and queens had food tasters back in the olden days. He watched the table of diners and people had finally started eating, no one falling face-first into their soup yet, so the food must be basically safe.

Apparently Ting's allergy was the only problem with the meal.

Kim leaned closer, her hand falling to his knee. "Do you think they suspect I'm an impostor?"

"Or is this a plot to harm her?"

"Either way, I can't eat it."

He covered her hand with his, allowing a second to reassure himself that whoever was threatening her—or Ting—hadn't succeeded for the moment at least. "I've got this one." He raised his voice. "Waiter. Waiter! Take this chicken dish away and get the owner immediately."

Before he'd drawn another breath, Mr. Chiang appeared at Kim's side. "Sir? There's a problem with the food?"

"A problem?" Marc allowed his frustration from the past hours to seep slowly into his words. "I should say so. Your staff was given a list of Princess Ting's preferences and medical conditions. That includes allergies. Your peanut dish there could have killed the heir to the Cantou throne."

Chiang paled whiter than the linen table cloth. "I have, uh, no idea how," he stuttered in seemingly genuine dismay, "this could have, oh my, happened. I will see that something else is prepared right away. Whatever you wish—"

Kim stood, waving her hand. "No need. I have lost my appetite. I believe I would like to gamble now."

Mr. Chiang wrung his hands. "Please, Princess, allow me to make it right for you. Our chef is the best in town."

Kim stared him down, blinking slowly as she studied him. Marc had to give Chiang credit for holding his ground. Kim pulled out the stops with that regal gaze, more intimidating than the brass dragons at the bottom of the staircase leading to the open upper level. Even knowing she was actually making a cop assessment of the situation, Marc found himself feeling a bit sorry for the casino owner.

Kim was a force to be reckoned with.

Finally, she nodded. "We will avail ourselves of room service later this evening."

A hint of pink flushed back into Chiang's face as he smiled his relief. "Thank you so much, Princess Ting. We look forward to making this right."

Kim turned her back on the casino owner in dismissal. "All right, Marc, are you ready to gamble?"

Something about her words kicked him in the gut. Gamble. His whole career was about taking risks on a regular basis. Why then did he balk when it came to pursuing his attraction to this woman?

He'd deluded himself with some nonsense about sex distracting him from protecting her. Yet the closer he stood to her, the less chance anyone else had of getting near her. After their history two years ago, he didn't have to worry about things getting serious.

So why not take a risk right here? Right now. They would both enjoy the hell out of it.

Marc palmed her waist low, right where the band of her panties would ride, panties that would undoubtedly be hot if her earlier satin-and-lace choice was any indication. "This whole weekend is one great big high stakes. Let's go for it."

Kim blinked fast, as if caught by surprise, then she tossed back her head, her hair shaking in a flirtatious dark curtain. "What's your pleasure tonight? Cards? The slots?"

Raising his hand, he flicked back a strand of her hair that caught on her lip gloss. "Lady's choice this evening."

Her lips curled in a smile, gloss shiny and begging to be kissed off. "Anything where the Joker's wild."

CHAPTER FIVE

AFTER AN EVENING SPENT checking out every corner of the casino, Kim had a serious case of falling arches. Dang, but she'd never wished for her butt-ugly cop shoes more than right now.

The elevator door dinged at the penthouse level, Marc still glued to her side. It felt as if they'd spent their time together today more intensely than they had in the month they'd known each other in Cantou.

They'd eaten Mr. Chiang's substitute meal, then rushed back down to scope out as much of the casino as they could, even managed a quick peek into Chiang's office. They hadn't discovered anything to advance the investigation that she could ID yet, unless she counted the fact it appeared the owner had enjoyed a romantic dinner with his current lady love—although the apparent cheapskate had served the woman the leftover peanut chicken.

She hoped all these seemingly insignificant pieces would come together soon, or she didn't stand a chance at winning the bet. Plus, the longer she spent with Marc, the more tempted she became to toss away something a lot more precious than a week's vacation. Something like, say, her self-control.

Inside the penthouse they had privacy to speak, now that her other guards had gone to their rooms for the night or stood in the hall outside the door. Thank goodness her people made sure the room stayed safe from and clean of bugs or goons. She yanked the spiky heels off her feet and tossed one to the floor.

Marc leaned against a wall. "You do the royal thing well."

She stared at the second shoe in her hand until realization dawned. "Oh, uh, how quickly I forget people have to pick up after me if I throw things down and leave them there."

Marc shrugged. "You do have your assistant—"

"Sun—"

"Right, Sun—for this job."

Kim thought of the days when she'd had a dozen servants to pick up after her. Too easily she could slip and become that spoiled child again. Right now, she craved the warm familiarity of her tiny apartment over this penthouse. She'd earned that space for herself.

She shook off the thoughts. This assignment had her in such a turmoil. Certainly not the time to fall under the allure of entering into a relationship again when her judgment might be shaky at best. "Sun's undercover, too, and will take it out of my hide once we're back at work if I give her grunt work, like picking up after me."

"Good point." He slid his formal jacket off and hung it on the back of a chair at the small table with the remains of their supper. His waist sported a 9mm strapped in a leather harness. "While you were calling the hospital to check on Vincent and Tim, I double-checked with Sun to see if she'd remembered to pass along the peanut allergy info. We had to check, and I figured she would be less insulted if the question came from me."

"Thanks. Good catch." She lined her shoes up in her closet, calling over her shoulder, "And?"

"She seemed genuine."

Kim hesitated in the door connecting her room to the sitting area, more than a little surprised at his distrust of one of her colleagues, but if he'd gotten a strange read off Sun's reaction, Kim wanted to hear more. Instincts were there for a good reason. "Seemed?"

He shrugged and resumed his post holding up the wall. "She even showed me your Preference List on her PDA. Is she the kind of person to tweak something after the fact to cover her ass?"

"She's new to the force here." Kim padded barefoot back into the room and sank into the sofa, then bolted up again, restless. "I don't know her that well."

"So that's a dead end, no matter what." His eyes locked on her, narrowed and dark, following her every move. "I think we've done all we can for the day, given we were chased by gunmen and nearly run off the road."

She rubbed her hands along her arms, pacing around the room, hands lighting on odds and ends for no reason at all. "I guess you're right. I'm just still so wired after all that's happened."

"Then we won't go to sleep."

Gulp.

That stopped her cold. What did two adults usually do to stay up all night in a hotel suite? She didn't see a board game or deck of cards anywhere. That left only one alternative that she could think of.

The word *sex* blared through her mind like the bright lights of a Las Vegas marquee.

She wanted him. No question about it. But she

could not handle the distraction being with him would cause. The feelings he evoked had scared the socks off her two years ago and things hadn't changed one bit. The precinct shrink told her she ignored problems rather than dealing with them.

Well, she preferred to think she saw problems and stayed clear of them until she had a plan.

Right now, walking racetrack circles around this room to get rid of her nervous energy seemed to be a plan. "You don't have to stay up with me. You're really carrying this bodyguard thing to the extreme. We've got Las Vegas's finest in the hall and all over the place."

"Maybe I'm wired, too." He shoved away from the wall. "Let's go out on the balcony and get some fresh air."

How had he known just the right suggestion for her jitters at the end of this bizarre day? Getting out of this place, out in the open air sounded heavenly—and they would be farther away from the tempting bedrooms.

His eyes narrowed. "Did your guys check the balcony?"

"I'm not sure." She reached under her dress to pull her gun from where she'd strapped it to the inside of her thigh, Marc already having pulled his 9mm from the waist harness.

The weight of the gun in her hand offered a sense of grounding, regaining control of her world. Her training, her job—here she knew the rules.

Slowly, he unlatched the sliding doors and nudged the glass to the side. She paced her breathing to keep her heart steady. No hyperventilating like she'd done on her first time out on the streets after the fatal shooting. She could hold herself together these days. Besides, the chances of there being anyone out there were slim but she appreciated Marc's thoroughness.

Not many men could hold a weapon alongside her. She lost a lot of dates when they learned how she made her living, and damn, now her brain had shifted to dating. What a time for that to happen as she walked out onto a romantic moonlit balcony with an attractive man in uniform. A bed wasn't necessary after all.

Think about the job.

Scanning the garden area, she didn't see any lurking attackers hiding behind sculpted bonsai trees or bamboo furniture. Dim lanterns on a wire creaked in the late-night breeze, casting enough illumination with the help of the moon and Las Vegas's neon lights for her to feel certain of her safety.

She lowered her gun. "Looks all clear to me."

Marc was slower to drop his weapon to his side, but eventually he joined her out in the open air, setting his gun on the table between two loungers.

Her toes curled on the warm concrete, the light wind easing the muggy night. She sank down into a lounger, stretched out her legs and relaxed her head back with a long sigh. "You are such a smart man. This is exactly what I needed to unwind tonight and recharge for tomorrow."

"Thanks." He dropped onto the lounger beside her, his white shirt a beacon in the dim light. "I figure we have a full day ahead of us, hopefully with no more attempts on your life, Princess Ting."

She flinched. "Don't call me that."

"Sorry." He stretched, shoving his hands behind his head while the street traffic hummed and honked below. "What made you decide to leave the country of your birth and all the shoe-picker-uppers behind?"

He'd struck a nerve larger than he could imagine with his Princess comment. He'd hit on a secret bigger than he could fathom, one even she sometimes forgot since she'd lived with it for so long.

How angry would the man beside her be if he knew the truth about how fully she'd left behind her heritage?

"KIM?" MARC SNAPPED HIS FINGERS in front of her face to nudge her out of her daze.

She seemed so far gone at the moment, she might as well be back in Cantou. She blinked fast, rejoining him in the here and now, with the lanterns and the buzz of cars below. "What was your question?"

He considered blowing off the whole discussion and just kissing her senseless, an idea with serious merit. Except he could tell she wasn't ready yet—the reason he had suggested they come out on the balcony to talk in the first place, so she would relax and then he stood a chance at getting physically closer to her.

"My question? What made you decide to leave the country of your birth and all the shoe-picker-uppers behind?"

"A few reasons. There is such political turmoil there. They're trying for democracy, but no one is safe. In case you haven't noticed, I'm not much into pageantry." She wriggled her bare toes. "I think I must have been a changeling child."

"Yet there's no mistaking the royalty in you."

Even in her bare feet, hair loose around her shoulders, she had the regal bearing.

Kim plucked at the stitching on her dress, swirls

of flowers over her that made him want to trace them—touch her.

Her restlessness continued. "I'm only a cousin."

"They just let you leave?" He thought they kept a pretty tight hold on the royal family members over there, but then as she'd said, the place was in turmoil.

"They had no choice. I'm an adult who makes her own decisions."

"Yet you still go home often." He figured she must feel strong ties to keep up those visits. Might she one day change her mind? That unsettled him more than it should. He only wanted an affair, not anything permanent. No more attempts at a trip to the altar for him.

Her eyes got that faraway look again. "Just once a year now. I go because I love my family."

"Even Ting?"

"Ting and I have a bond." Her fingers stilled and she finally looked at him. Stared at him, her pupils dilating in a mutual longing he couldn't miss. "Shouldn't we." She paused, cleared her throat and started again. "Uh, shouldn't we turn in and rest up so we'll be fresh in the morning to look for diamond brokers rather than looking *at* each other?"

"Yes, Your Highness."

"Don't call me that." Her eyes snapped with anger. "We're not on display, so there's no need."

"Just calling it as I see you." He couldn't resist needling her. Why did she insist on denying who she was? She could be Kim Wong, American cop who happened to have Cantou royal blood. As he saw it, she didn't have to choose between the two.

Except expressing that opinion would be counterproductive to what he wanted—to kiss her. Antagonizing her would not put her in the mood.

He swung his feet to the side and leaned his arms on his knees, angling closer to her. "The first time I saw you in Cantou, I couldn't look away."

She turned her head to face him. "Hmm... I remember. Even after you persuaded the guards you didn't mean to nearly tackle me at the fruit market, you didn't try to feed me some corny line like so many guys do. You weren't intimidated by the whole royal thing, either. You just asked me out to lunch."

"I remember. I was there."

She laughed, low and soft, the sound riding the breeze, and just like two years ago, he couldn't look away. Screw waiting. He had to taste her now.

He leaned forward and captured her lips.

Strawberries. How could he have forgotten that her lip gloss tasted like strawberries? He damn well wouldn't forget that detail again. When he'd stolen that quick kiss after her shower, she hadn't put on her make-up yet, so there'd been no strawberry gloss to taste. Now he had to find out what else he'd forgotten about the taste of Kim…if she would give the okay.

She sighed, her hand drifting up to tease along the back of his neck. All the encouragement he needed.

Hand plunging into her hair, he parted her lips with his tongue and searched deeper, sweeping inside for a more intimate kiss. He definitely wouldn't lose the memory of the feel of her at this moment. How he knew, he wasn't sure. Somehow their time together now was more vibrant than before, on high speed, high energy.

Because of the life-and-death stakes of earlier today? Of the barracks horror?

Maybe. He was a different man than he was two years ago. He'd learned the precarious nature of life, a tough one for flyers taught to believe they were invincible. He was still working to put the different perspectives together, but he did know he wouldn't miss out on pursuing the chance to be with Kim this time.

He skimmed his hands along her waist, hauling her closer until the soft curves of her breasts pressed to his chest. He wanted more. The soft whimpers in her throat indicated she felt the same.

"Kim." He nipped along her neck, up to her ear. "Share my bed."

She flung her head back to give him better access. "Is that a question or a command?"

"Could I command you?" His roving hands stopped just below her breasts. An inch higher and he could fill his hands with her.

She clamped her fingers around his wrists and looked him in the eyes with a wry twinkle, the fog of passion there, but slowly replaced by a sense of reality. "Try it that way and see how it goes for you, big guy."

He laughed against her damp lips. "Then consider it a question, one I've asked before on more than one occasion, if I recall correctly."

"Your memory is perfect and you know it."

"And you still haven't answered yet."

"Marc, I've only just seen you one day." She eased back her answer with a sigh, a hint of reality sliding into her eyes. "One very intense day, packed full of adrenaline."

"We knew each other well."

"Two years ago. Sure, we have some history, and I won't lie." She pulled his hands from her but linked their fingers together and set them on his thighs. "Yes, I'm attracted to you, and I assume from that kiss that the feeling is mutual, but that doesn't mean it's right to follow through on that attraction."

The proverbial splash of cold water made its way over him. This night wasn't going to end the way he'd hoped; however, he would take heart in the fact she hadn't closed the door completely. "I take it you're saying no, but you should consider the fact you'll be safer if we share a bed. I can guard you better."

She chuckled low and long. "You're such a man. That just proves you'll use any excuse." Another laugh slipped free. "I'll be sleeping in my own bed. Leave the door between our rooms open if you're that concerned. You'll be as close as across the room, and don't forget I'm a cop. Come in unannounced and you very well might get shot."

A woman who could take care of herself. He had to admit he found that hot. Marc stood, their hands still linked. He tugged her to her feet so she faced him. He couldn't resist stealing one last kiss, no lingering, just a quick brush, her strawberry gloss long gone but the taste of pure *Kim* still very much there and too damn enticing for him to let the kiss go on much longer.

"Goodnight, Marc," she whispered against his mouth.

"Night, Princess."

Letting go wasn't easy, except he reminded himself the weekend had only just begun. Yes, they had an investigation to complete. Except the way he saw it, getting closer to Kim and solving the case weren't mutually exclusive. Tomorrow was a new day. Kim's assistant undoubtedly had a schedule for them to follow.

But Marc had plans of his own.

CHAPTER SIX

KIM FOUND WAKING in the morning to an empty bed all the tougher when she'd made out with a hunk the night before.

Sending him off had been tough. Really tough. Having him insist they keep the connecting door open didn't help much, either. She'd jerked awake at least a million times, jarring at the sound of him rolling over or snoring ever so slightly in his sleep.

Scrubbing the sleep from her eyes, she grabbed her BlackBerry from beside her bed and scrolled through her messages. A few messages from friends—and an interesting snippet of info from Captain Pearson that she couldn't wait to run past Marc.

After she brushed her teeth and hair.

Three minutes later, she raced to the connecting door to Marc's room and knocked on the door frame, tugging her overlong Dodgers' T-shirt to her knees. His bed was empty so she walked in.

"Marc?" she called just as he stepped out of his bathroom with a towel around his waist.

Ah man, sometimes life just didn't play fair. The broad expanse of his muscled chest was sprinkled with dark hair that just begged for her hands to sweep over it to brush away the droplets of water. If she didn't have a day's worth of investigative work ahead of her, would she indulge herself?

She wouldn't know because she did have a job to do.

Kim clenched her hands as added insurance against temptation and stepped into the room as if it made no difference to her if he flat out dropped that towel. "I just heard from Captain Pearson. They found some hidden financial records for Mr. Chiang and he's in debt up to his eyeballs. His lifestyle *looks* normal, but when you dig deeper, he's got two mistresses."

"Ah, two money pits."

"Pretty much. One has a suite here and another has her own condo downtown."

"Pricey." He reached into his duffel bag and pulled out a pair of boxer shorts, khakis and a black polo shirt. "All the more reason to give credence to the diamond scam and lay the blame on Chiang's doorstep."

"But we've got people watching every inch of this place, even the vault, and nothing's moving so far." She tore her eyes off his hands choosing clothes. Would Marc actually dress in front of her? Rather than risk finding out, she spun on her heel and turned her back to him to give him privacy to dress while they talked. "We've even been watching the women's jewelry—mine, too."

"Yours are paste. I checked," he said, the rustle of clothes accenting his words. "Even that weighty outfit you wore to the casino on the first day."

Kim fidgeted, finding that hearing him dress felt just as intimate as seeing him step into those boxers. "That was more beading than rhinestones."

"Sure, but there are all sorts of expensive jewels and precious metals that can be used as currency." He paused for the length of time it took for a *zip*. "I actually know a bit more about jewels than the average layperson. My mother made and sold jewelry—another reason why I was a logical fit for this assignment."

"All a good starting point for the day." She didn't hear any more noise from behind her, but she didn't want to turn unless she knew for certain. "Are you, uh, finished dressing?"

Now she did hear sounds. His footsteps padded

along the carpet, closer and closer still until she could feel the heat of him behind her.

He lifted her hair and pressed a long, slow kiss against the vulnerable curve of her neck. "I'll meet you for breakfast in a few minutes, Princess."

"Uh-huh." Wow, what a stunning response, but she couldn't push much more past her hormone-stunned brain after that mind-numbingly hot kiss. She could only walk ahead into the sitting area to wait for him, when it hit her....

She'd never found out if he'd been fully dressed or not.

AFTER BREAKFAST and stuck in the middle of a day scheduled to the microsecond, Marc could understand how this royal family stuff could get old fast. He was already in the mood for some serious alone time in a cave. He'd had enough of being managed to death by an agenda. Not to mention followed by photographers, an assistant, protective detail and all-around sycophants.

At least the next item on the list of activities afforded them a hint of privacy. Marc eyed the man-made creek that wound through the casino, complete with boat rides. Hokey, sure, more along the lines of an amusement park sort, but he would do just about anything to spend five minutes alone with Kim.

Sun was playing her assistant role a little too well, it seemed. Did the cop have another agenda that made her want to keep Kim occupied? Or was Mr. Chiang with his pair of mistresses at the root of all of this? The currency was reputed to be moving through his casino, after all.

Marc was considering which one to set up an "accidental" chat with first when the overly solicitous casino owner appeared at their side.

Mr. Chiang flourished a minibow to Kim with a predatory gleam in his eyes. "Your Highness looks especially lovely today."

"I would thank you for your compliment, but I'm afraid my boyfriend is the possessive type." She nudged Marc's foot.

Mr. Chiang turned his attention to Marc. "Not very politically correct these days."

Marc wanted to point out that keeping a couple of women on the line and flirting with another wasn't all that politically correct—or moral—either.

Kim hooked her arm around Marc's. "What can I say? I am drawn to his alpha male personality."

She leaned in to whisper into Marc's ear. "That part was not acting on my part, even though I can't figure out why because half the time I want to slug you."

Marc couldn't help but throw his head back and

laugh, even though Mr. Chiang looked none too happy at the intimate exchange. Just a flash of anger that cleared away as apparently the smart businessman within took control over the libido. "I hope you both enjoyed the special meal our kitchen sent up to the penthouse last night."

Memories of the heated kiss that came later slammed through him. If they could just clear away this damned diamond-smuggling case, so he could have Kim to himself for a week of leave time...

Kim elbowed him in the side, reminding him to talk. "Yes, thank you."

She nodded that regal head of hers, the jeweled ornament holding her hair behind her ear, dangling with the movement. "Your chef outdid himself."

"I will relay your compliment. And many thanks for allowing us the chance to redeem ourselves."

"Our pleasure." In more ways than one.

Chiang backed away. "I will leave you both to enjoy the rest of your romantic ride together. I hope you will tell your grandmother about all the amenities of our establishment, so that we may see her if she makes a trip to the United States."

"Of course."

Inspiration struck Marc fast and bold. "Sun,

why don't you talk to Mr. Chiang to get the recipes from last night's meal so we can send it on to Ting's grandmother?"

That would give the undercover cop time with the casino owner—and give Marc some much needed breathing space, because having the assistant in the boat with the two of them served no purpose to the investigation. The boat rides had a driver in costume, so they couldn't talk about the investigation anyway.

Beside the flowing water, Marc extended his hand to help Kim settle into the small boat before he sat next to her. The small canoelike craft with a yellow tiger head on the bow lurched forward. Their driver—a man with a paddle who pretended to row even though the boat ran on a rail just barely submerged under the water—stood in front of them.

"So you like alpha males."

"When you are a woman in my position," she said, neatly veiling her words in double meaning so the driver would hear "princess," whereas Marc knew she meant "cop," "it is difficult to find men who are not intimidated."

An invitation if ever he'd heard one.

He tucked a knuckle under her chin, tipped her face to his and brushed his mouth over her glossy lips. He could get addicted to the taste of strawberries.

Two years ago he'd thought she was special. Now there was no denying the fact that this woman rocked his senses in a way that nobody—not even his ex-fiancée—had before. In fact, he could have sworn the boat was tipping…. He jerked himself from Kim's allure because, damn it all, the boat lurched to the side, pitching them into the chilly waters.

And cranking machinery.

"OUCH!" KIM SHOUTED, dodging Marc's probing hands checking her for injury a half hour later back in their suite.

Talk about feeling undignified. Falling ass over elbow into knee-deep water, but stuck wedged between the boat and the side getting all soggy…

Chiang had been mortified.

Her entourage had swarmed her with weapons drawn.

She looked like a dripping wet dog right now. A polka-dot puppy, thanks to all the bruises.

Paparazzi camera flashes had gone off like crazy. No doubt there would be photos at the precinct to document the moment. She would never live it down.

She and Sun had decided it wasn't a genuine attempt on her life since there hadn't been any real danger. Only humiliation.

Marc lifted her elbow.

Kim jerked. "I said ouch and I meant ouch!"

"I'm just checking the bruise on your arm to make sure you haven't broken anything."

"Trust me." Kim charged past him into her room, pitching her heels into her closet. "Nothing's broken but my pride, which is as bruised as my butt." Her teeth chattered, the damp clothes clinging to her body. "I wish we could get them to turn off the air conditioner."

She pivoted around to find Marc an inch away. Before she could speak, he scooped her up in his arms.

"Marc!" she squeaked. "What are you doing?"

Although his arms felt so warm and good around her she couldn't bring herself to tell him to stop. He carried her across the sitting area, through his room and into his bathroom.

Oh. My. Goodness.

She should say something…. Her brain went on stun.

He set her on the floor and turned on the shower. His intent heated over her a second before the steam started to roll from the water.

She chewed her lip. "This probably isn't a wise idea."

"I know."

"I'm really tired of making wise decisions, though."

"I understand what you mean, but it still has to be your choice if I stay to enjoy this shower with you or not."

She saw the same hunger in his eyes, but he waited for her. The decision *would* be hers. Yet, the last thing she wanted to do now was think. She could steal this private pocket of time with him, the moment when no one would be looking for them. She was tired of living her life for others. This moment was for her and for Marc.

"Yes," she whispered, arching up toward him, mouths meeting, tongues tangling. This need had been two years in the building.

Apparently he didn't need any more encouragement than that lone word.

With urgent fingers, she peeled the wet, black polo shirt from his chest, the same broad expanse she'd been aching to touch this morning. His hands roved down her back. The simple touch caused her to sigh into his mouth.

He slid the zipper of her dress down in a long, slow *zip* that reminded her of earlier when he'd so seduced her by dressing while she kept her back turned. He gripped the hem of her dress and bunched the fabric up, up, up in his hands until he swept the clothing over her head and off, sending it flying into the sink.

"Ah, Princess," he groaned, "I do so like your lingerie choices."

For a man who'd claimed to like her emerald lace bra and thong set, he sure got rid of them quickly enough, soon to be followed by his own pants and boxers until they stood naked together and he plunged them into the hot shower.

Yes, that felt more amazing than anything she could recall. Although she wasn't sure which was hotter, the sheeting water or Marc's skin. He teased her breasts with his fingers, his mouth, the heat of him pressing against her stomach until she thought she couldn't wait any longer.

Hadn't they both waited long enough? Two years, after all. They could go slow the next time.

She slid her hand between them and stroked him, languorously. "No more waiting."

"So now you command me. And I don't mind one damn bit." He reached out of the shower and grabbed his pants, tugged his wallet free and…a condom appeared in his palm.

Kim swiped it from his grasp and sheathed him,

while his hands continued to skim over her, stir her higher and higher.

Then Marc pressed her against the shower stall wall, plunging up into her, filling her with a wonderful thickness. Her skin tingled with a sensitivity that made every bead of water dart over her with an added brush of pleasure.

She hitched her leg up over his hip. His low growl of appreciation shot a thrill through her just as he gripped her other leg and helped her lift it, locking her feet behind his back.

Their water-slicked bodies moved against each other, closer, deeper while they both whispered frantic litanies of want to each other between kisses and nips and caresses. She arched harder against him, desperate to find release. Even as another part of her wanted this to last…she shied away from the word *forever*. A scary word.

She scrubbed that from her brain just as he grabbed her hips and helped her find the right angle to wring…

Her head flung back. Marc pressed urgent kisses along the arch of her neck as she bit his shoulder to keep from calling out and risk bringing any guards into this steamy haven. Water sluiced over her in rippling waves that matched the satisfaction surging through her.

Her legs slid down in a boneless heap, her arms and his wrapped around each other all that kept her from falling to the shower floor. With him buried deep inside her, aftershocks of bliss still shimmering through her in microbursts, she fought reality edging in to steal these last moments before she would finally have to tell him the truth.

Because without question, this changed everything.

"YOU KNOW, THIS CHANGES everything," Marc said, grabbing for the big fluffy robe to pass to Kim, as much as he regretted covering the view.

But he couldn't think straight with that view in sight, and the time had come to talk. They wouldn't have long before they had to rejoin their scheduled commitments for the rest of the day.

"I realize that. How could it not? It was…so much more than I expected."

Thank goodness they agreed on that. He hadn't realized how much he needed to hear her acknowledge that until the words passed her lips. Even if she had stuttered on the words.

Marc tugged on a pair of sweatpants. "That scares you?"

He couldn't stop himself from pushing.

She hugged the robe closer around her, "Losing control is always a frightening thing."

He reached to pull her onto his lap for a long and silent moment. "What happened? With the scar on your shoulder, I mean."

She tucked her head under his chin. Dodging his gaze? "A near miss on the job. The bullet grazed me." She paused. A sigh shuddered through her. "It hit my partner. He didn't make it."

Marc's arms convulsed around her. He'd thought they had something in common, that moment with the drawn guns, searching the balcony, and when he'd thought about her surviving assassination attempts. However, he'd had no idea how very much they actually did have in common.

"I'm so damn sorry." He held her closer. "I mean it when I say I do understand, in the way that you understood when I told you about Rubistan. My fiancée walked last year because she couldn't deal with the stress of this way of life. No doubt, it's tough as hell. There are just no words that will ever make it all right, but it means a lot having someone who's there for you."

She didn't answer, a slight sniffle the only sign she'd heard his words, but it was enough, because yes, he did understand. So he kept right on holding her and letting her hold him back until her muscles relaxed against him again.

Kim eased away, looked up at him and caressed his scarred jaw. He expected to see a smile. Too bad life never seemed to dish out what he anticipated.

She had a huge frown on her face. "There's a problem, though."

"Problem." Of course. He should have seen it coming. "Fine. If you want this to be a one-night stand kind of thing, just say it now. I'm not in the mood for a repeat of my engagement where she drew things out."

"No. No! It's not that kind of problem." She slid off his lap and plowed her hands through her tangled hair. "Things are complicated."

"Aren't they always in relationships?"

She stopped in the middle of the room and waved her hands around her face. "Ting and I truly do look so very much alike. When we were little we used to get such a kick out of confusing people by swapping places."

"The princess and the pauper," he prompted, trying to follow her conversational leaps.

"Sort of, except there was no pauper, more of a cousin who didn't have quite as much money and power."

"You don't seem the kind that it would matter to anyhow."

"I'm not." She paced restlessly. "We only had our grandparents alive because of an avalanche during a skiing trip that took our parents when we were ten."

"Damn. I'm so sorry." Where was she going with all of this? "I can see why you would want to leave a place with so many sad memories."

"Me, yes, but not my cousin. She lived for the attention, the jewels, the pageantry. The money."

"Then I guess it's luck you were both born as you were."

She stopped pacing, the frown gone, the regality there for him to see.

There for him to see.

The truth hit him between the eyes so clearly he couldn't believe he'd never guessed before. He only had one question left unanswered. "When did the two of you decide to switch places, Princess?"

"I switched from being Princess Ting to being the royal cousin Kim at fifteen and never regretted it for a minute."

He exhaled hard. The rest of the truth gut-kicking him. He'd fallen for a princess.

Fallen hard. As hard as the furniture that crashed to the floor in the next room.

Someone had broken into their suite.

CHAPTER SEVEN

KIM JOLTED. "DAMN IT," she whispered. "I left my gun in the next room."

Marc snagged his from the bathroom vanity. "Stay behind me, then, for backup if we get into a close fight."

"Got your back." She appreciated that he hadn't tried to relegate her to the closet or under the bed. She could grow quite attached to a man who respected her strengths, because no way could she have let him go out there alone.

He meant far too much to her. Wasn't that why she'd really pushed him away before? So nobody would shoot at him the way people shot at royals? Except people *did* shoot at him no matter what, and wow, things were a tangle in her mind at an inopportune time.

Marc eased the door open, gun poised and ready. He peered around her into the sitting area…and shook his head. *Nothing there.*

Her heart pounded in her ears. She knew intellectually that no one could hear it but her. Still it almost drowned out her ability to hear what went on around her at this critical time. She refused to allow flashbacks from her past to distract her even more—the sickening showdown that led to her partner's death.

She pointed to the connecting door to her bedroom that sat propped open an inch. The intruder could have moved into that room. In fact, he or she very likely could have if Kim was the target.

He nodded. Padding slowly across the carpet, he made his way toward the door while she followed closely, wishing she had her gun so she could sweep around and enter from the other door. Wishes were a waste of time.

Like wishing she had told him sooner about being the real princess. And like wishing there had been time to hear his response to her revelation, because it chewed at her insides wondering if he would reject her now, after they'd made such amazing love together. She'd run from the life of royalty—the paparazzi, the materialism and, yes, the obligations. Might Marc be put off by the possibility those could still bleed through into their lives?

She needed to shove aside these distracting thoughts and focus on the moment.

Marc creaked the connecting door open and stepped back, waiting for the reaction from the room....

"Kim?"

Sun's voice echoed from the other bedroom.

Kim exhaled and stepped around Marc into her room. "Sun? You scared me to death, creeping in like that."

Her fellow undercover cop stood by the king-sized bed with two costume boxes, her PDA resting on top. "Sorry. You were gone so long, I was starting to get worried. The costume ball dinner is due to start soon, and you and Marc hadn't picked up your outfits."

Kim couldn't help but feel the curious scrutiny of Sun's gaze sweeping over the robe and Marc's sweats.

Marc strode boldly into the room and took the two stacked boxes. "We were going over some points about the investigation before changing. Thank you for bringing these up. We'll be down shortly."

Kim stifled a smile. His take-charge attitude came in handy sometimes. She slid her costume box off the top, passing Sun her PDA. "Anything new from the precinct?"

Sun shook her head. "Sorry. We're on our own

here to figure this thing out with what we've got so far."

"All right, then." Kim clutched the box. "What will you be wearing tonight?"

"I will be dressed as a barmaid."

"Got it. See you there," Kim said, walking her toward the exit.

Once the door closed behind her, Kim sagged against the wall and looked at Marc. "Do you think it's just coincidence that she was in my room?"

He spread his hands. "You know her better than I do."

"And I barely know her at all." Not a reassuring notion at all, especially when they had to go back downstairs into a huge gala of masked guests where anyone could show up.

The image of that security nightmare barely formed before her earlier tangle of thoughts about assassination attempts and her fears for his life threatened to unravel in her mind. What a time to realize she—a woman who could stand down crooks on the street—had been holding back from committing her heart out of fear. She'd told herself she needed to stay out of relationships, because she was really a princess and that wouldn't be fair to bring all that baggage into a relationship.

But the real baggage was her fear. Her fear that

someone she loved might die—of an assassination attempt or of a fluke avalanche. Throwing herself into her job and new life was so much easier. How crummy to figure out she wasn't any better than his fiancée who'd walked a year ago.

Because Kim knew right here, right now, she was totally and completely in love with Marc.

MARC WASN'T MUCH FOR COSTUMES. He knew his Joker call sign came about because of his lack of a sense of humor and he was all right with that.

He wasn't all right with wearing a Zorro costume. Marc touched Kim's hand in the crook of his arm as she stood beside him in her pink fairy-tale princess attire. They'd been in this damn receiving line for over two hours. How this advanced the investigation, he couldn't see.

No wonder Kim had wanted to check out on the royal lifestyle. There must not have been a minute to call her own growing up.

A waiter tapped Marc's shoulder and motioned for him to step back to make way for a food cart. His stomach rumbled. He'd bet there was no peanut chicken on the menu tonight.

He wished they could have five minutes to talk so he could figure out why she'd avoided him right after Sun had brought their costumes. He vowed right then and there he would make sure to find that time. No more running from relationships.

When he got back to his home base in Charleston, South Carolina, he would put in for a transfer here to Las Vegas so he could be near Kim and pursue her for real. He would make time. Damn straight what they'd shared earlier had changed everything.

He reached to pat her hand on his arm again...and her touch was gone. He started to call for her and remembered at the last second to use her undercover name, oddly enough her true name. "Ting?"

Marc looked beside him, but she wasn't there. Where the hell had she gone? She wouldn't have just left without telling him.

He searched the crowd for Kim—he could never think of her as Ting—in her princess mask and gown. He saw just about every costume known to womankind, even one that looked remarkably like that cross-dressing cop from the police station yesterday. Still, no Kim...

Then wait. He caught a glimpse of the poofy skirt heading toward an exit door. The body size looked right, the piled-up hair, the curve of the face. Yes, the costume seemed perfect...except wait.

That fairy-tale princess wore blue and he could have sworn Kim's costume was pink.

"WHERE IS YOUR GOWN?"

Her gown? The raspy whisper echoed in Kim's head, as well as the stairwell she'd been hauled into by a lady pirate with a gun. The ammonia scent of freshly mopped tile threatened to gag her.

Just as Kim had feared, the melee of the costume ball had provided too good a cover for someone bent on snatching her. She didn't dare fight against the biting grip on her arm, not with a gun pressing deeper into her side by the lady pirate. Just her luck, a waiter had distracted Marc for a split second and turned his body out of her reach.

Apparently the lady pirate had been waiting for that instant.

How had the gun even gotten past all the metal detectors? There had to have been a breach in security—or this was one of their own. The hoarse whisper did a decent job at disguising the woman's voice, but Kim had the sneaking suspicion already that Sun hadn't dressed as a barmaid after all.

However, letting the knowledge slip would sign Kim's death warrant, considering they'd already used lethal force on her informant. She had to play this smart. Calm.

"What gown?" Kim asked, trying to buy time as the woman dragged her down the stairs, her high heel catching as her captor wrenched her arm higher behind her shoulder blades.

She shoved Kim toward an exit sign glowing in the dimly lit stairwell.

If they made it outside, that would be the end for her. Kim walked as slowly as she dared while working to sort through the questions.

"The one you were wearing the first day?"

"I put it in a box and I assumed the cleaning staff took it. It had a hole in it, anyway." She scanned for possible escape routes. If she could get free, maybe she could reach her gun strapped to her leg, but the bulky costume made it a difficult reach at best.

Surely someone would have missed her by now. They would be searching the floor area, bathrooms. How long before they checked the stairwells?

She could smell the woman's fear beginning to seep through her costume. Hopefully she would panic and make a mistake soon.

"My people took that one and had it examined. The beads and jewels were nothing but paste and tin."

"Yes. So?" What did they expect?

The exit door creaked above them, from where they'd started, sounds from the casino wafting in. Kim's hopes rose—her fears did, too, for whomever might unwittingly be stepping into harm's way. Yet strangely, the gun didn't waver from her side.

"Where is the real gown?" This question didn't come in a raspy whisper at all, but from their newcomer and the last voice Kim had expected to hear.

The voice of her cousin.

Kim couldn't stop herself from jerking against the gun as she spun to see what she could barely believe to be true…. Her cousin descended the last two steps to join them.

She peeled off her mask just as Kim did. Sure enough, it was like looking in a mirror, the only difference being the image staring back wore a blue costume instead of pink.

Her cousin glared. "I want my cut of the money and you had better turn it all over to us." She stared past Kim. "Sun, what have you found out?"

Wow, her cousin gave up her cohorts mighty easily. It sure didn't pay to do business with her.

A dirty cop explained so much. Scooter's murder. How her route in the limo had been leaked that first day.

Sun's panic radiated off her in waves as she

pressed the gun back into Kim's side. Damn. Not surprising, Sun had lied about her costume, too, as an extra cover.

The traitorous cop's hand shook. "I'm still trying to sort through it all. She's tricky, though. Why don't you see what you can get out of her?"

Her cousin tossed aside her mask and leveled her gun at Kim. "Being a princess just doesn't pay what it used to. I've had to join up with some—how shall we say?—less than savory sorts to make enough to keep myself in the manner to which I have become accustomed."

Kim sorted through this bizarre turn of events…. Her cousin showing up here, now, in the middle of a search for illegal jewels. "You can't mean this. How can you do this to our grandmother?"

She considered a reach for her gun or dodging to the side, but any way she looked at it, she was one person against two guns. If only she could take her cousin one on one and kick her butt seven ways to Sunday, like she'd done once when they were kids fighting over a schoolboy crush.

"Our grandmother actually believes we should scale back our lifestyle and stop making so many appearances. She thinks it is time to let the new democracy slide into place." Her cousin shuddered. "I will not give up so easily."

Kim wanted to cry to think of what she had let happen through her own selfish need to escape. What a time to realize how she had been running from more than just her role as princess, but from her true feelings for Marc. No longer could she run from life. And she figured it out right when she could well be seconds from death, judging by the cold ruthlessness in her cousin's eyes.

No. She couldn't let that happen. Not without telling Marc how much she loved him. To do that, she needed to figure out what the hell was going on here.

Searching for the real gown? The first gown. Realization dawned. The first vintage costume, the one she'd worn in the limo during the chase, when Marc had to tear apart the skirt. She'd left it at the police station and Pearson somehow found an emergency replacement. As far as she knew, the first dress was still in a box at her precinct.

Sun had been sent ahead to the casino on Friday morning before the brief so she wouldn't have been at the station to notice the costume change. Now she had to get free to call the station and let Captain Pearson know he had a mint in jewels—and likely silver-and-gold studs—stored away in a cardboard box in his office.

If she died here, her cousin could take her place

all too easily…. She wouldn't put it past her if she would try something like this. And Sun might figure out the truth about the dress swap. The exit door swung open again. A flash of light sliced through the dim stairwell from above.

Her cousin's gun swung toward the opening.

Toward…

"Marc!" Kim shouted in warning, wrenching out of the pirate's grasp. Too late.

The gun fired.

Kim didn't have time to reach for her own weapon. She launched at her cousin while Marc plowed toward the lady pirate, pinning the high-seas maiden to the floor. He was still moving, but that didn't mean he hadn't been hit.

Kim chopped at her cousin's gun arm and shoved the palm of her hand upward on the impostor's nose. Blood spurted. Her cousin shrieked and clawed at the air. Kim downed her in a flurry of taffeta and screams.

From the corner of her eye, Kim could see Marc hammer the pirate's gun hand against the floor. Again. Again. Finally, the weapon skittered away. He peeled Sun's mask off, his movements appearing fluid. Easy. Blessedly unharmed.

Flipping her cousin to her stomach, Kim pinned her hands behind her back as the doors burst open and the undercover cop detail poured through. Better late than never.

She glanced over at Marc, who had not even a scratch on him, and smiled. She looked around at the scene, princesses, a Zorro, a lady pirate and an entourage of other costumes to make for the strangest bust ever. Marc winked. Her Joker, only hers.

And who said he didn't have a sense of humor?

SAFELY BACK IN THE PENTHOUSE suite sitting area, Kim knotted the fluffy robe tie around her waist, glad to have cleared away the fairy-tale princess costume and all the crooks for one night. Her cousin and Sun were being processed down at the station now. Kim had placed a call to Captain Pearson to check on her first costume—and sure enough, the thing was loaded with at least ten million dollars' worth of jewels and precious metals.

Her skin itched all over again.

She flopped on the sofa. No doubt, she would have a tiara painted on her locker when she got back to work. But then it was time for her to blend the two halves of herself. Hadn't her grandmother been trying to teach her that all her life? Or at least until she'd ditched her true identity. It was past time to visit the older woman and make peace for the grief that the deception had nearly wrought on her home country.

Her cousin would go to jail and Kim would acknowledge her true lineage again—while keeping the name Kim. She could never call herself Ting, since she had embraced a life she'd worked hard to earn with her new name.

Hard work, something her spoiled cousin knew little about. The moment the police had showed up, her cousin had begun crying for special consideration and deals, looking woefully pathetic with her big fat tears and broken nose. She would turn over all the names of her higher-up connection in the jewel racketeering scheme. She would do anything for a lighter, softer sentence. Kim didn't doubt her cousin would land on her feet and the case would be sewn up tight.

Only one problem remained.

What would Marc think of this final turn of events?

As if he heard her need for him, he filled the doorway from his room. He leaned against the door frame, making sweatpants and a T-shirt look mighty fine. "Now that we've finished with your buddies and the protective detail has cleared out, while you're getting dressed, do you want me to hail you a cab for home or to the station?"

She toyed with the belt on her robe, suddenly in no real hurry to claim her prize in the bet with her two friends. "I should probably go to the station and process the paperwork. Two of my detective friends and I have this bet going as to who can crack their case first. Except now that I look at things through the whole life-and-death filter of tonight's events, the bet feels—" she groped for the right word "—unimportant."

"What was the prize?"

"Vacation days."

"That's prime." Still, he didn't move toward her, leaving the next move up to her.

"Honestly, what I'd like to do most is stay here in the suite, since we have it for the night, and talk to you." She took a risk, because if she didn't, she would regret it forever. "To be with you if you still want me, and I think you do."

"You know I do." His words came out in a tortured growl, but still he didn't move closer. "First, I think we need to clear up a few things."

Ah hell. When she'd taken the risk she'd been so hopeful, almost certain…. "Things like what?"

"This princess thing. You said you've never regretted it. You're sure you meant that? Because

I've got this pal who quotes Shakespeare a lot, and one of the sayings comes to mind right now. 'The lady doth protest too much, methinks.'"

"And you would be right." When she saw what her cousin could have done to their country... "I can't simply wish away who I am." She could see how some men wouldn't want any part of that. Would her decision cost her the man she loved?

"Now that the secret's out, what does this mean for you?" His dark, soulful eyes that always stared straight at her, only her, never ceased to turn her inside out.

"There's going to be a big to-do in the papers, given the world's fascination with royals. I will probably do a preemptive interview with my preferred reporters. It'll be rough going for a while, but eventually things will settle down. Then I won't have to return to Cantou more often than once a year if I don't wish." She tried to be honest while making it something he could live with, because she so very much wanted him in her life. "There will just be more pageantry when I do. And I will probably get a lot of ribbing around the precinct."

"We may have a problem here. I'm damn sure not prince material."

Oh my. To be her prince someday, they had to

be… She smiled and rose from the sofa. "I believe that's all a matter of perspective."

He strode toward her and looped his arms around her waist, her prince every bit as hunky in a sweat suit as he was in his formal uniform. "Does your perspective include dating me seriously, even if I'm not particularly princely material?"

"Wow, you certainly do cut right to the chase." She grinned up at him, her heart galloping in her chest.

"I'm a serious man, always have been. It's been two years and I haven't gotten over you. Believe me, I tried. Obviously I didn't do a good enough job convincing anyone, since my very smart ex-fiancée figured it out and ran. I think two years of failing to forget you speaks for itself, Kim. I'd like to get a transfer here so we can spend more time together and explore what we feel for each other."

Two years of thinking about her? That did tweak at her already softened-up heart. She stroked his scarred jaw, a reminder of how precious every day of life was and how she shouldn't waste a second more. "You're a tough one to forget, too."

"So you've been thinking about me?"

"Yes. More than I could even admit to myself until I saw you again. Then when the guns all started coming out down there tonight and I thought I could lose you…" Her head fell to rest on his chest and she allowed herself a moment to let all the fear seep through her, because even as she cherished every second, the thought of losing him did scare her so.

"Uh, you're not going to walk, are you?" By the gruffness in his voice, the prospect of losing her bothered him every bit as much.

"I'll admit that for a second there, my heart squeezed so tight. I had this flash moment of what it would be like to close up shop on loving anyone ever again." She caressed along his scarred jaw again. "That moment turned very, very dark and I found no safety in hiding in that darkness anymore. You've taught me how to be the princess and the cop and the woman who loves you so very, very much."

His arms tightened around her as his smile dug trenches into his face. "I like the sound of that."

"Risking love is scary for me and I imagine it's scary for you, too, not that men seem to be as comfortable admitting to being scared as women are." She winked. "But I'm willing to take this risk with you. We're worth the payoff. So, yes, I love you and I would very much like it if you moved to Las Vegas."

He tipped her face up toward his, brushing a kiss over her lips once, twice, and no doubt soon to be many more times. "You won't be sorry, Princess. I'm certain. Because with a love this strong, you're gambling on a sure thing."

To Catherine Mann and Debra Webb—
thank you for being so much fun to work with!

THE WILDCARD

Joanne Rock

CHAPTER ONE

"OH MY GOD. YOU'RE DRUNK on the job."

Sergeant Dorian Byrne of the Las Vegas Metropolitan Police Department rested her aching head in her hands at her friend's bald statement of the facts. Leave it to fellow detective Kim Wong to get straight to the point.

Thanks to the wonders of three-way calling, Dorian had contacted the officers she was closest to on the force for advice on her current predicament. She wobbled unsteadily on her high heels at a pay-phone booth while using her cell phone's headset. Although her friends had joined her in a bet about who would close their case first this weekend in a city-wide sting operation to clean up the casinos, Dorian knew Kim Wong and Clarissa Rivers would never want her to lose because she was under the influence.

"Let me get this straight," Clarissa chimed in from her operation across town at the Free Throw

Casino where she was working on an illegal gambling ring. "You think someone's been spiking your water and you didn't even notice it tasted alcoholic?"

Dorian fought the urge to pound her slightly spinning head against the pay-phone booth wall in the lobby of the Pompeii Hotel and Casino. She was scheduled to pull a final stint of undercover work at the Pompeii to ensure an all-encompassing set of arrests on a local crime network, members of which were abducting area prostitutes to sell as sex slaves abroad.

She had to pull herself together if she was going to accomplish her goals.

"You know how awful the water can be in this town. I didn't order bottled because I think it's a frivolous expense for the department." She couldn't help a financial conservative streak that came from growing up poor. "So I loaded up my water with lemons from the bar to make it more palatable. I probably drank four glasses this morning while getting acquainted with the layout of the casino."

"And you think there was alcohol in all of those glasses?" Kim's accent came through a little more pronounced since her cover at the Great Wall Casino had her playing into her Asian heritage while she investigated diamond smuggling.

"If there was a little alcohol in each it makes sense I'd be tipsy by now and explains why I didn't notice at first, right? After the first drink, I thought I felt funny because I didn't get enough sleep last night, but by my fourth glass, the effects were too obvious to deny." She tried not to panic at the thought that someone in the hotel already knew her identity and drugged her because she was a cop. Could her cover already be blown?

"You don't think you could have been drugged with anything besides alcohol, do you?" Clarissa sounded worried. "Should you get to the lab and have them draw your blood?"

An oath slipped out of Dorian's mouth, her reactions slower and less professional.

"I never thought of a drug. Damn. I can't get a complete chemical analysis of my blood three hours before I have to meet my partner for this operation." Her head swam as dread grew at the thought. If only she didn't have to be working with Simon Ramsey this weekend.

The trouble he'd once caused her made being drunk on the job seem like a picnic.

"Don't panic." Kim lowered her voice. "Save the tainted water by bringing the last glass up to your hotel room, and you can send it to the lab after you make your arrests. You don't have time to track down a nut screwing with your drink right before the biggest arrests of your career. Captain Pearson needs these kidnappers caught." Kim's bottom-line assessment made sense. "Besides, Special Agent Ramsey will be there backing you up to make sure you don't make any poor judgment calls."

Oh God. Dorian refused to admit that Simon himself had a detrimental effect on her judgment.

"In the meantime, you need to go to your room and brew about three pots of coffee from the little java maker." Clarissa must have been standing next to a slot machine, because the sound of electronic binging and bonging came through the airwaves as loudly as her voice. "You can always snag a few extra coffee packets off a maid's cart to be sure you're not getting anything contaminated from room service."

"Good idea." Perking up at the solid direction to see her through the next few hours, Dorian clutched her water glass to her chest as she peered around the Pompeii's main casino floor. "I'm going to stumble my way back to my room and I'll send you both a text message, so you know I arrived and wasn't carried off by the kidnappers stealing prostitutes."

She hadn't dressed in her most provocative

clothes for her cover as a lady of the evening yet, but she'd gone with a shorter skirt than usual while she cased the casino this morning. Somebody watching her might think she was a new working girl who would be easy to steal.

Her stomach turned over unpleasantly.

"You got it," said Kim. "I'll check my phone while I'm stuffing myself into the traditional Cantou garb. Does anyone know the point of a Mandarin collar when it completely restricts your Adam's apple?"

Snickers followed as they all said goodbye. Dorian swallowed back the wave of nausea-tinged nerves and hung up the phone before she made her way to the elevator. She just hoped the coffee and some exercise would clear her head before she had to get serious about her cover tonight. She'd followed this case for too long and dreamed about the missing call girls for too many nights to let a vicious ring of black-market slave traders steal even one more victim for their brutal brand of cruelty.

No wonder men loved women who wore lacy merry widows and silk stockings with garters, Dorian thought to herself later that afternoon. She had to be a freaking contortionist to fasten the last few hooks on her black corset, complete with plunging neckline.

Hot, frustrated and battling a hangover headache, she stared into the hotel room mirror at the glammed-up stranger in do-me lingerie. A degree in criminal justice and seven years of training and experience in law enforcement had led her to this—a push-up bra and red lipstick.

And wasn't that a testament to the success of the women's movement?

You've come a long way, baby. Too long to end up walking the streets in stilettos and a miniskirt. Dorian slid into a tailored menswear jacket to hide the cleavage show until she reached her destination downstairs on the Pompeii Hotel's casino floor—now that she had her head screwed on straight from the alcohol scare earlier. She'd called the station to find out how to package her water glass and the remains of her drink for chemical testing Monday morning. For now, she had a case to close by using her body as bait.

"You almost ready, Dorian?" Her radio crackled to life on the bed as she stepped into her shoes. The police dispatch system calling through to her would want an update on her progress, and by now, she was damn ready to get down to business. Whoever had tried to slow her down by tampering with her drink would be as sorry as the sadistic bastards stealing unsuspecting women.

She didn't have an LVMPD partner for this operation since her department had maximized manpower to cover as many assignments as possible this week. The city had been strongly urging the department to clean up the growing crime stats before tourism started to taper as a result. Dorian's captain had been working his way toward an ulcer due to the added pressures of his job, giving him no choice but to spread out his resources and pair his best investigators with what backup he could find. That's how Kim had ended up in one casino, Clarissa in another and Dorian still another. Their common goal to make serious arrests on their cases in progress had been solidified with the bet that whoever filed her report first would have the next week off.

The competition helped liven up difficult circumstances and potentially scary arrests. In Dorian's case, she would be teamed with the one man she never wanted to see while half-naked again. Hardly a coincidence since her life had a handy knack for operating under the principles of Murphy's Law.

"Dorian here." She answered the radio call as she hurried around the king-size bed decorated in extravagant gold-toned Italian linens. "I'm leaving now and will be downstairs in five minutes. I have my phone, but the radio is staying in the room."

"I'll inform your contact, Dorian. Good luck."

The hiss of the airwaves died, fading to silence the way Dorian's heart would when she got downstairs and laid eyes on Simon Ramsey for the first time in a year.

One year since Simon had walked out on her after she'd made the biggest mistake of her life with the federal agent his colleagues had nicknamed Wildcard. Her emotions had been off-kilter at the time, but she still couldn't believe she'd let a lousy week on the job drive her into the arms of Wildcard Ramsey.

All things considered, strolling through the Pompeii Casino in her lingerie wasn't that bad by comparison. Even if it meant experiencing twinges of regret on too many levels. Some that had to do with Simon. Others that originated much deeper in her past.

At least today she'd have the chance to vindicate the prostitutes disappearing steadily from Vegas this year. Sadly, the trend had gone undetected for a few months since many of these women had been marginalized because of their profession. But legalized prostitution in Nevada ought to entitle working women a certain degree of protection, and Dorian intended to be sure they received it.

Although, if Simon Ramsey thought that meant she'd be tossing her pride at his feet again, he was about to receive the wake-up call of his life.

LOOK HER IN THE EYES.

Be the first one to speak.

Make the apology the first words out of your mouth.

Simon reviewed his survival strategy as soon as he got the call that Dorian was on her way to his rooms. The Bureau had booked a high-roller suite for him under an assumed name—Simon Rainier—to give more credence to his cover as a West Coast card shark, in town for the weekend to gamble and look for girls to take back to L.A. He'd decided to extend that cover so that he could also act as Dorian Byrne's pimp to ensure her safety during a dangerous-as-hell assignment. But it was that part of the role that pissed him off every time he thought about it, since no man in his right mind would ever share a woman like Dorian, let alone pimp her out at a profit.

He hadn't been worthy of her a year ago, and for all his faults, at least he'd been on the right side of the law at the time. Now he had to pretend to sell her to any jerk-off with enough cash to pay for the favor?

This was one fake persona he'd have to struggle to maintain. As much as he regretted what had happened between him and Dorian in the past, he resented this approach to busting up a crime ring even more.

A knock at the door pounded in time with the quick jump of his pulse at the thought of seeing her again. He knew those quick and efficient raps were hers, the sound as straightforward and direct as she'd always been.

God, he missed her.

Reminding himself about the eye contact and the apology as he pulled open the door, Simon broke the first rule within two seconds. His gaze plummeted from her face at the visual shock of so much black and red—the bold, direct colors well-suited to a face more striking than pretty.

Her short, dark hair was cropped in soft waves around her ears with one long curl draped over her brown eyes. She had vaguely Latina coloring that gave her a perpetual golden tan, a feature he hadn't noticed as much in her usual grays and blues. But this afternoon she wore the shortest black skirt imaginable, short enough to show off the tops of her stockings. Short enough that if she bent forward just a little, anyone standing behind her would get a delectable eyeful.

"Nice to see you, too, Simon. Can I come in?" She arched a dark eyebrow his way, her painted red lips pursing at his rudeness.

No damn wonder. By now he'd broken all three of his self-imposed rules for this meeting and he hadn't even gotten around to cataloging the full extent of her.

"Please." He opened the door wider, wondering how to mend fences enough to get their job done.

The temperature dropped a few degrees when she walked by him, freezing him out with a look that men in the doghouse know well. And frankly, Simon had done his share of time there thanks to more women than he had any right to mess with.

He'd been up-front with women about playing the field before he met Dorian, but she'd cured him of that particular hunger from the moment they'd met. She'd been the lead investigating officer on a particularly gruesome murder scene when he'd shown up. She read him the riot act about local jurisdiction before excusing herself to lose her breakfast in the bathroom. Two minutes later, she'd emerged snapping a stick of gum and railing at the Bureau for interfering. He was hooked.

Too bad they shared exactly nothing in common aside from attraction. Dorian had made her feelings clear about his wild ways—on the job and off—and she seemed hardwired to resist his every attempt to win her over except for one incredible night.

"Look, I know I'm probably the last guy you wanted to work with on this detail, Dorian, but—"

"Save it, Ramsey." She moved slowly through the living area of the luxury suite, her gaze taking in the photos of the Strip and framed prints of Monte Carlo, before she turned and inventoried the frescoes on the majority of the walls. "You know I'm too much of a professional to care who I work with as long as the job gets done. Even if I get stuck with a Fed."

She turned to stare out at the Strip. His suite was only five stories above ground level, while he knew she was on the eleventh floor. Her view was probably better, but the luxury of this suite was lavishly over the top, like so many elements of Vegas. There was a minibar beside the hot tub built for eight and round-the-clock, in-room massages. Simon had received comped tickets to a handful of events over the weekend, too—not just as part of the suite, but also as the hotel's way of steering his investigation toward areas where the sex crimes ring operated.

The Pompeii was eager for the police to start making arrests on a case that was costing them business, and Dorian had received a solid tip that another kidnapping attempt would be launched this weekend. Local prostitutes were disappearing and—according to Dorian's information—being sold as sex slaves to rich men who fancied seeing American women helpless. From their brief phone calls to set up the sting, Simon knew Dorian couldn't wait to bring down the bastards.

"I just wanted to apologize for sprinting out last year. I wasn't in a good place back then." Major understatement.

He leaned against a marble-topped bar stocked with complimentary liquors bearing labels he'd never be able to afford out of his own pocket.

"Me, neither." She turned to face him, her arms crossed tight over the tuxedo jacket covering a hint of red lace and high breasts. "So why don't we agree to write off the whole awkward scenario as a bad idea? Then we can get down to more pressing concerns."

He didn't really want to write it all off since he hadn't offered up any kind of explanation, but then Dorian wasn't the kind of woman who would give a rip about excuses. She was already pulling a piece of paper out of her jacket pocket, her attitude all business despite the sex-minded attire.

"Do you really think hookers dress that well?" The comment leaped from his mouth before he could suppress it. Not that he usually did much suppressing of his thoughts, but he'd planned to be on better behavior.

At another frosty look, he tried to back up his point.

"It's just that we don't have much time to set up your cover, Dor, and we need as much believ-ability for your character as we can get. If you look too high-rent, don't you think it'll tip off the regulars that you might not be what you seem?"

The piece of paper she'd been holding landed silently on the polished black marble bar.

"Might I remind you, Agent Ramsey, that we aren't conducting a sting on a street corner in West Hollywood? Prostitution is legal in this state, if not inside the casinos, and some of those working women have made a very nice living from the proceeds. The Pompeii is a first-rate luxury hotel, and the women who risk the wrath of security to advertise their services here dress with that in mind. Trust me, I didn't just pull the first thing I saw out of my closet today. I researched."

He released a whistling sigh, wondering if they'd be able to work together peaceably after all.

"Okay. My bad." He peered down at the paper she'd taken out to show him—a map of the casino—and was only too glad to talk about their strategy for the weekend. "Are you sure the Abundance Thoroughfare is the place to target our guys?"

The hotel had been laid out based on historical snippets about the city of Pompeii in the years before the volcano destroyed a flourishing culture. The center of the hotel mirrored an actual ancient marketplace of the same name.

Simon had been briefed on her angle of the investigation—sex crimes were a growing concern to local police. But the FBI had gotten involved when a racketeering case they'd been following started sharing key suspects with a ring allegedly responsible for the disappearance of local prostitutes. Five women had gone missing in recent months, and Dorian uncovered evidence the women had ended up overseas, hooked on a variety of drugs and being used as sex slaves by wealthy men until the women were eventually sold into brothels. The market for this kind of thing was small, but apparently demand for American women was steady.

Simon's agency had been working with CIA operatives overseas to get the missing women back home, but he would be more directly involved with shutting down the operation on this end. Months of investigative work had led to this weekend, and he wouldn't blow it by letting his personal history with Dorian get in the way.

"I think it's a good place to start." She traced the narrow line on the map with one vermillion-painted fingernail. "Most of the shops lining the marketplace are legitimate, but there are a couple that remain questionable."

Her nail slowed as she reached two Xs drawn with pink highlighter.

"You said they have women right in the booths?" Simon hadn't ever been the kind of guy to spend a lot of time in casinos, preferring to take risks in career-related venues so he could tell himself his recklessness served a greater purpose.

"The proprietors say the women are models, and certainly plenty of vendors use live models to showcase their wares. But the two I've highlighted have no accounts with local modeling agencies. I even quizzed agencies on both coasts, and no one has ever sent girls to the Pompeii Casino to work for either of these places."

He weighed that information as he studied the vaguely erotic frescoes on the wall behind the sofa, depicting a Roman maiden's tryst with a laurel-wearing guy in a toga. There wasn't a lot of nudity, but the way he held the woman with his hands venturing everywhere while the lady squirmed was definitely suggestive.

"These chicks just walk around the booths doing nothing?"

"They wear watches or belts being sold by their supposed employer, but their togas are pretty risqué. I thought maybe I'd hang around and see if anyone tries to…buy my time. Ultimately we see if we can gather any information on how a larger-scale kidnapping effort might be going down. We need to spend some time with our ears to the ground."

"So that's your end of the job for tonight. How do I fit in?"

"To start with, you'll keep an eye on things to make sure I don't get sold off to some sadistic billionaire, but later you'll give me a believable cover so that I can retire from the casino floor on your arm and maintain the appearance of a big-ticket item."

Something didn't add up.

"Are we sure that gels? I know you've been covering the sex crimes angle longer than me, but does it make sense for a good pimp to take his best seller off the market for himself?"

"Who said anything about a pimp?" She folded

her arms under cleavage that refused to be covered by her jacket.

"I—don't know." He'd never survive this job unless he looked somewhere else when he talked to her. He'd avoided shared investigative work for twelve whole months, but he hadn't been able to hand this job off to anyone else.

"Legalized prostitution has all but put the old-school pimp out of business in this town, Ramsey. No self-respecting big earner on the Strip would bow down to some horn-dog man's authority just so she can have the privilege of giving half her money away to a dope user who's only looking out for himself."

"I'll be damned if I know how I could have hit a hot button during a conversation about pimps." He couldn't even come close to figuring her out. "I assumed that would be my role in all this to give me a legitimate way to hang out with you and still make connections that would help my side of the investigation, too."

"Well, you're *not* my pimp."

"Since that's settled, do you care to share with me what role you'd like to see me play besides watching over your shoulder?"

With most any other local cop, he would have dictated the way they'd handle the operation, but he'd seen Dorian work before and knew she brought a lot of investigative smarts to the table.

She leaned a shoulder into a decorative Roman column separating the living area from the kitchen of the suite. A fresco of the Roman god Bacchus languished over her head, his arm looped about the shoulders of a curvy servant who seemed to be falling out of her toga.

"Since I can't work this assignment with a pimp who acts like he owns me, I think you ought to pose as the john who wants to buy me." She arched a speculative eyebrow in his direction. "It might be a stretch to pretend you want me, but you're a pro, right? Make it work."

And wasn't that just the way of a woman? She might feed you all the right lines about putting the past behind, but in the end, she made sure you never forgot your mistakes.

With Dorian intent on avenging her pride, this was going to be one hell of a weekend reunion.

CHAPTER TWO

IF REVENGE WAS PETTY, why did it make her feel so good?

Did that make her a petty female? The thought tormented Dorian as she strode through the miles of hallway leading to the Abundance Thoroughfare inside Pompeii Casino's subterranean shopping area. Private card games populated the rooms on either side of the faux street, the gathering of modern merchants made to look like a Roman marketplace complete with bright silk awnings and woven shopping baskets for browsers.

Maybe working with Simon this weekend wasn't such a bad idea, since she obviously had a few unresolved issues where he was concerned. They'd shared a good working relationship at one time and she owed it to this job—and to the mission itself—to repair things between them.

"Dorian?" His voice from behind forced her to slow down.

"Yes?" She checked out the terrain and wished they didn't have to speak to one another here—in plain view of the marketplace where they should have their covers nailed into place ASAP.

He nodded toward an open supply room with a maid's cart out front. The room was full of towel racks and bins of mini hotel soaps, shampoos and lotions. She didn't mention this had been the same storage space that had supplied her with extra coffee for her unexpected intoxication earlier.

Slipping into the unoccupied space, she figured anyone who saw them would think they were zipping inside for a quickie, a scenario that worked well with the cover. But then Simon had always been good at thinking on his feet.

"I know you've been up in arms every time I make a suggestion, but I gotta toss out one more comment because there's no way you've got the walk right."

She stared hard at him, knowing what he was saying but not ready to give in to Simon being right just yet.

They were in a too-small space that forced her to really see him in a way she hadn't back in his spacious suite. He had West Coast good looks from his blue eyes to his square jaw and his surfer-dude scruffy haircut. His brown hair had been sun-bleached at the ends for as long as she'd known him, even though there were sure as heck no waves to ride in Vegas. Something else must keep him outdoors and…fit. At an even six foot he had one of the most remarkable bodies she'd ever seen on a law enforcement guy. Not all bulging muscles like the workout freaks who filled the local gyms on the weekends, but lean and toned, solid and strong. He could outrun any of the muscle heads, and that was a big-time plus in this business.

"Dor? You know what I'm saying?" He stalked even closer in their tiny room, oblivious to her corporeal line of thinking.

Thank goodness.

"I've got the walk wrong." She repeated the gist of his issue, knowing he had a point and that she had to snap out of it.

"You're motoring through the building like a cop on a mission," he informed her with a lowered voice. "I think you need to slow down and add a little more hip action."

She knew exactly what he meant, but recreating that walk was going to come at a high price. Damn this stupid job. Blinking, she waited for her old ghosts to scatter so she could move ahead.

"I think you lead with your hips, actually." Simon frowned, staring down at her pelvis as if he'd come upon an unsolvable riddle. "Have you ever seen those models on TV where their hips come down the runway before they do?"

"I've got it. I'll straighten out the walk."

Her eyes burned for an interminable second before she forced herself forward. She'd do the walk in the hotel corridor, not in a supply closet with her audience of one.

"I know this has to suck for you." Simon's unexpected insight made her pause.

"What do you mean?" She froze.

How would Simon Ramsey have any idea what made this assignment so tough for her?

"Any kick-ass woman would resent hiding her strengths behind a camisole and garter stockings. I know you've gotta feel fairly—uh—naked to the world parading around the casino like that and I think it takes major guts."

He didn't know the half of it, and for that, she was grateful.

"It does suck." She pushed up her sleeves and gritted her teeth in what she hoped would pass for a smile. "Thanks for noticing."

She started out the door then and ran straight into a tall, bony older woman in a gray maid's uniform. The woman's lips pursed tight with disapproval as she took in Dorian's outfit.

"This room is off-limits to the public." The maid's holier-than-thou stance was full of judgments and assumptions.

"Don't worry, I didn't steal any of your soaps." She winked as she shouldered past the woman. "I don't have anyplace to hide them in this outfit."

Immersing herself in her cover with newfound zest, Dorian strutted down the hall, letting her hips lead the way just like Simon suggested. She wouldn't let hangovers, old grudges or judgmental maids distract her from what she'd come to the Pompeii to do. No matter what happened this weekend, she would be nailing the people who were taking advantage of women trying to make a living in impossible circumstances.

IT HAD BEEN A BIG MISTAKE to accept this assignment.

Simon watched Dorian flirt openly with some yahoo in a Stetson and alligator boots two hours later and tried to swallow enough of his frustration to do his job. She'd flipped some kind of internal switch after their supply closet chat, and ever since then she had absorbed the call-girl role and made it her own. She practically oozed sex as she stroked an idle finger along her collarbone and batted her long eyelashes at Tex.

Had she ever looked at Simon that way? It ate him up that he couldn't have celebrated their night together the way he'd wanted to. But he'd been deep undercover and violating every kind of professional protocol by being with her at all. He'd only flown to Vegas for a day to report in from some casework in L.A. By all rights, he should have told Dorian he was leaving town, but his brain had been muddled by a lousy case and the two glasses of Scotch she'd insisted on buying him when he met up with her at a dive bar where he'd never expected to see her.

Sleeping with her when he hadn't been totally aboveboard ranked high on a long list of personal stupid moves, especially when he knew she'd refrained from dating him because of his reputation as a wildcard.

Damn.

When Tex's hand slid around her waist to the small of her back, Simon's fingers curled into a fist at his side. He walked away from the display of imported watches he'd been browsing and veered closer to Dorian and her grope-happy friend.

Faking an interest in the jewels at the booth closest to where she stood, Simon eavesdropped on her conversation with the scum-sucking cowboy.

"I'd love to hear more about the party." She spoke in a breathless voice women usually saved for sex.

The wispy tone sent a shot of heat straight to Simon's groin.

"Why don't we head somewhere more private and I'll tell you all about it," Tex drawled, his voice lowered to ensure privacy. "In intimate detail."

Dorian giggled as if that was the most amusing suggestion she'd ever heard. Simon braved a glance their way to see the stranger's hand moving south on her hip.

The bastard. The guy's fast hands were ticking Simon off more with every inch they traveled. He took deep breaths to cool the red fog falling over the whole scene as he watched them together.

He shouldn't interrupt yet. Not unless the jerk tried to take her somewhere else. But oh man, it wouldn't be easy to just stand here much longer.

"Hey numb nut, you got a problem?"

Several beats of Simon's heart passed before he realized Tex had been talking to him.

He'd been caught staring like a drooling kid at the video game store.

"Yeah, I do." Never one to back down from a challenge, Simon brought over that bravado to any cover he might adopt. His supervisors could only expect him to fake so much.

"It's okay, baby." Dorian ran her fingers up one side of Tex's cheek, attempting to draw his attention back to her. "He can look but he can't touch without my say-so."

But Tex wasn't that easily swayed and he swung his big shoulders toward Simon in a blatant invitation to make something of it.

"Well, bring it on, pretty boy. I can settle your problem in about ten seconds."

The guy's raised voice drew stares, and Simon could tell from a glance at Dorian's face that she was none too pleased over his interference. He'd tried to let her handle it. Really he had. But wasn't it his job to watch over her?

"I don't think so." Thinking fast, Simon shuffled aside the cover she'd suggested for him, knowing he needed more clout to put this guy in his place than a competing john would offer. He stepped closer to Tex and lowered his voice. "If you want a piece of her, you need to see me first. Understand?"

Tex appeared confused for a second before comprehension dawned in his eyes. He removed his hands from Dorian's butt, much to Simon's satisfaction. Simon nodded meaningfully toward a quiet corner off to one side of the busy market, and the two of them walked away from the shopper's thoroughfare to do business. Dorian didn't protest, but he knew that was only because of the role she played.

He'd figure out a way to get the information on the party from Tex without having to send Dorian into his hotel suite. He just hoped his efforts would be rewarded with a measure of forgiveness from Dorian, because the woman sure did stare daggers into his back as he walked away.

"WHAT THE HELL was that all about?" Dorian exercised great restraint not to tackle Simon the moment he walked into his hotel suite three hours later.

Three. Hours. Later.

After Simon had disappeared with the best lead she'd had on her case, she'd smoothed over the ruffled feathers of the women who ran the booth that sold jewelry and leather goods as a cover to promote local prostitutes. After Dorian nailed the bigger criminals in the ring selling women abroad, she'd be making other arrests around the Pompeii, including the bogus leather goods folks who expected a piece of the action any of the girls received while at their booth. Until then, she couldn't make waves.

After that, she'd canvassed the hotel on her own

to drum up more information, finally retiring to her room and then—after another hour passed—filching a key to Simon's suite from the front desk with the help of a call from her captain. She'd gone from furious to worried and back again.

"It was about getting information from a good lead before the guy turned so horny he couldn't talk straight anymore." Simon bolted the door to his suite, locking them into the privacy of his decadent room. "Do you have a problem with that?"

Damn the man for being so confrontational. With any other guy she worked with, she could voice a gripe without it exploding into World War Three, but Simon had always known how to push her every last button.

Some buttons, she recalled, had been very pleasurable under his touch. But when it came to messing around with her investigation, she was less impressed.

"Yes, I have a problem with that." She marched across the room for the showdown, unwilling to concede this point after his Lone Ranger ways had caused her extra worry, work and stress.

"Why? Were you hoping Tex would feel you up in the middle of a public venue? How much longer did you expect me to wait before I deflected the guy?"

Simon met her midway across the living room, the two of them engaged in an angry stare-off so quietly intense she could hear the sounds of their breathing.

"I can handle myself and you know it. But instead of letting me redirect the guy, you had to barge onto the scene, playing white knight to destroy my credibility with the women who pony up the cash for that booth on the mall week after week." She stood close enough to breathe in the scent of him, close enough to remember exactly why she'd fallen into his bed a year ago.

And didn't that say a lot about a man's appeal when a woman could still want him even when she was this mad at him?

"What do you mean?" He crossed his arms and spread his feet apart in that "king of the world" stance men sometimes took.

The posture pissed her off more than it should have, but wasn't that indicative of her whole problem with him? He couldn't share control to save his life. Oh, he'd made surface attempts in the past—like earlier today when he'd agreed to the role of a john—but when push came to shove, he expected to get his own way. Two hours into their shared assignment he was already breaking team.

"I mean that most of the working girls in this

town don't have pimps. It's a benefit of legalized prostitution that hookers don't need as much protection as they might in some other places, and a lot of the independent earners look at women still connected to a pimp as sort of low class and antifeminist."

"Antifeminist?" He had the nerve to quirk a smile.

"Yes, damn it. And don't you smirk at me when you don't understand squat about this end of the operation. Women operate differently from men. We have social hierarchies and complex relationship structures. Thanks to you, I'm now at the lowest end of the totem pole."

She didn't bother pointing out that she wouldn't be privy to much inside information if the women in the business all stared down their noses at her. He knew that as well as she did, even if he hadn't bothered to show the least bit of remorse about the fact.

"Lucky for us both then, I wasn't dealing with a woman when I asked Tex to step aside. We both said exactly what we were thinking, no bullshit social structures getting in the way. And wouldn't you know, even with my testosterone-impaired communication skills, I still managed to find out that the party he wants you at tomorrow night is probably a mass viewing of women for potentially 'unlimited' work down the road." Simon turned on his heel, pacing the polished tile floor as he shrugged off his jacket, his body silhouetted by the fresco of Bacchus on the wall behind him. Bacchus didn't come close to measuring up.

Dorian stared at Simon's shoulders shrouded in an ice-blue silk T-shirt and tried to focus on his words.

"Unlimited work? He said that?" She tried to envision the slow-talking Southern boy who'd propositioned her being involved in the darker crime of selling women on the black market. "Could anyone possibly connect sex slavery to unlimited prostitution? At least hookers get paid."

"I don't know. Tex—says his name is Matt Gaines, by the way—he tried to make it out like the party would have a lot of high rollers who like to impress each other with their taste in women. He implied the most coveted females get passed around and go home with the fattest purses."

Dorian shuddered. "Did you call in his name yet to run it for past arrests? And do you think he's being up-front about the party?"

Simon moved toward the laptop open on the desk and hit a few keys.

"I'm entering the name now to see what happens, and it's tough to say whether the guy was telling the truth. He sure seemed intent on getting you there, even though I warned him you'd charge full price for each new…uh…taker." He looked up at her from over the top of his computer monitor, his eyes inscrutable.

For a moment she had the impression that this cover might not be so easy for him, either. The possibility spoke to emotions about Simon she thought she'd paced long ago. Emotions she couldn't afford to feel now with so much riding on her ability to remain focused on the job.

"So you're okay with me attending a party behind closed doors with multiple alleged sex offenders, but if I talk to one in public in full view of a busy shopping area, that's too dangerous?" She retreated into the safer mode of verbal sparring, an arena where she could at least pretend she didn't care about him.

"I bought my way into the party, so you won't be alone." He pointed to the computer screen. "I've got nothing on Matt Gaines yet, but I took a photo of him on my cell phone when he was talking to a waitress. I'm going to submit the photo and see if that yields any hits."

"You *bought* your way into the party? The FBI must be backing you with one heck of a budget for this trip." She had to admit she would appreciate having him with her in a room full of horny men who thought they could buy sex. Still, that wouldn't even be as bad as men who thought they could *force* women into sex, which could very well be the case if the party was a front for the more sinister crimes taking place in Las Vegas.

"The city is raising holy hell about the bad press. You know nothing loosens bureaucratic purse strings like political pressure."

She knew all about the political pressures since her police captain had been working eighteen-hour days for the past two weeks as a result of it. As much as Dorian wanted to help clean up Vegas for personal reasons, she also needed to come through for Captain Pearson, who was working himself into the ground.

"Does that mean maybe we'll get some extra backup?" Something about the private party context made her uneasy. The event would be tough to police.

"I think the LVMPD will have to provide the backup resources since my department is strapped, working on the overseas efforts to get those other women back." He stopped suddenly. "Are you okay?"

She hadn't realized he was watching her, but his

sudden question made her start. Some of her emotions about this case—about those women suffering abroad—must have shown on her face.

He pushed out of his chair before she could respond.

"I—" She waved him off, choked up by stupid old stuff and afraid he might see more vulnerability in her eyes. "It's nothing. Just the kind of case that gets under your skin, you know?"

She couldn't quite look him in the eye, training her gaze out the window at the lights on the Strip as the sun sank low on the horizon.

"I know all about those kinds of assignments."

His words surprised her, as did his movement to stand beside her at the window. He gazed out at the view with her instead of forcing her to meet his eyes. To reveal secrets she wasn't ready to relinquish.

"You do?" She'd always thought of Simon as an expert at not taking his work too seriously. "I thought the Wildcard was always game for anything."

"You remember that night we hooked up?"

She blinked to follow his line of conversation, surprised he'd bring it up now.

"I remember it, all right." What started out as a painful day in her professional life turned out to be the most memorable night of her personal life. Right up until Simon pulled the morning-after vanishing act.

"I was knee-deep in a case gone to hell, and you hadn't seen me in a while because I'd been on extended assignment to L.A." He turned to face her now, his expression shadowed in the growing twilight.

Had that been the case that had been rough for him? Maybe he'd been as off his game that night as her. The thought chinked away at the barriers she'd put up against him.

"I didn't know anything about your caseload." But she had noticed he'd been out of town a lot. Somewhere during Simon's full-throttle courtship, she'd started volunteering for any jobs that might bring her in contact with Bureau guys. Simon had worked hard to win her over and, damn it, he had.

That caring had made it suck all the more when she'd woken up to an empty bed.

Simon drew in a breath and blew it out slowly.

"I was only back in town to meet a contact who never showed. When he didn't arrive, I figured I was free for just that evening, but I had to jet the next morning because—technically speaking—I was working undercover that night."

CHAPTER THREE

SIMON HAD NEVER BEEN the intuitive type when it came to understanding women. But then, it didn't take much sense to interpret the dawning horror in Dorian's eyes.

"Going home with me was part of your *cover?*" Her cheeks flushed deep pink like the blush that he'd once seen steal over her whole incredible body.

Except this time, that rosy color wasn't a good thing. She looked ready to throttle him.

"No. Yes. That is, I'd wanted to be with you for a long time, but I wouldn't have approached you that night if it didn't fit with my…er, character's reputation."

This was going to be tougher than he thought, but he couldn't continue to work with Dorian if they couldn't get past what had happened between them. They had to trust each other this weekend or the consequences could be deadly.

"Let me guess. You were a player."

"Among other things." He'd thrown himself deeper into that role than any cover he'd ever taken. "I was trying to gain the trust of a handful of L.A. business partners who seemed to be hiding a hell of a lot of income behind some investment properties and a struggling casino out here."

"Since when do casinos struggle?"

"The FBI's question exactly. All the business partners had ties to organized crime, and we thought I might be able to connect the dots for some arrests." He shook his head, remembering the fiasco and hoping his experience might help Dorian feel better about whatever was biting her in the butt about their current investigation.

There had to be more to it than just their one-night stand for a dedicated cop like her to be so upset about him working the pimp angle, or checking out on him mentally when they were following up on a good lead. He'd worked with her on homicide cases in the past where she'd spent two minutes hurling in the ladies' room and then thirty-six hours straight chasing down leads and hauling in suspects.

If he didn't know better, he would swear she was holding back on this one.

"I'm going to ignore the fact that you slept with

me to make yourself look good to your criminal friends and concentrate instead on why it all got under your skin."

He'd seen that direct stare of hers before, usually when she wanted to wrangle information from a reluctant suspect. Her brown eyes were tinged with gold and yellow, cat's eyes that were beautiful and also a little unnerving when she watched you so steadily.

Pivoting on his heel, he retrieved a couple of energy drinks from the minibar. He handed her one before cracking open the top on his.

He dropped into a sofa angled toward the window and rapped the cushion beside him in invitation. They sat side by side in the dark, the neon colors of Las Vegas reflected around the suite in a carnival glow. Dorian took a sip of her drink, her soft scent filling his nostrils as she folded her legs underneath her. He diverted his eyes from the way the movement hitched up her skirt, knowing he couldn't afford that kind of distraction now.

"I slipped so deep in that cover some of the guys at the Bureau said I wasn't ever going to come out." Those rumors had stung when he'd found out about them afterward, his reputation as a loose canon cemented after that case. "It wasn't true, but I did form a connection with the crew I sold out—so much so that I lost a lot of sleep over the ethics of the whole thing."

"What kind of connection? You liked those guys?" She sounded surprised but not judgmental as she settled an arm along the back of the couch.

"It's different when you stay undercover longer." He knew she'd done short stints for a day or a weekend before, but FBI work lent itself to longer, more specialized operations. "You have to find legitimate ways to relate to your suspects or you'll never gain their trust. No one is a hundred percent evil. They have kids. Families. They like baseball or their pet dog, and you find a way to connect to that. Then, well, you've created a solid relationship with a criminal. It tends to mess with your mind."

He quieted the guilty niggle of his conscience that reminded him he was working hard to regain Dorian's trust. To make a connection. Did his expertise in that area give him unfair advantage?

"So you form false friendships to leverage information." She nodded. Understanding but not understanding. "The more they trust you, the more you unearth for the good of the investigation."

"That's how it began." He remembered all too well the feeling of triumph that he'd won his way into the innermost circles. "The problem was I got off on the job a little too much. There's a sense of loyalty among people who've committed dark deeds together, and the guys I fell in with—they'd do anything for each other. That kind of brotherhood is rare and I started to understand how gangs can recruit so effectively. It becomes the family you never had."

"You genuinely liked the crooks?"

He couldn't tell if censure lurked beneath her surprise.

Shrugging, he tried to lighten the implications of the admission.

"They operated with a code in place. No violence toward women and kids. The worst thing I ever saw those guys do was take out a kiddie-porn trader, and I had to admit, my morals weren't all that offended." Although God knows, he'd questioned himself about his ethics after that one. "Bottom line, I made the busts when the time came, but I know how some investigations venture a little too close for comfort."

He leaned back on the couch and waited for her response, hoping she'd own up to whatever was bugging her on the prostitution assignment.

"You can't beat yourself up for being effective at your job."

"Quite a credit to my character, isn't it?"

"You are a character, that's for sure." She shook her head as if he was a lost cause, but she smiled, too.

The attraction to her still kicked him hard. He couldn't be around her and not notice the magnetic draw of her strength, her commitment to the job. He admired her for that selfless hard work to a job with little glory and a paycheck that would never make her rich.

He should have let her in on his case last year before he'd bolted from her bed.

"Dorian?"

She opened her mouth to speak, perhaps sensing the direction of his thoughts, or maybe to clear up her misgivings about their case. But before she could say anything, his computer chimed with the sound of incoming mail.

Damn.

"You think that could be a hit on Tex?"

"I don't know, but I'd better take a look. Whatever it is it came to my work e-mail."

She was too much of a pro to hang over his shoulder while he checked, but she rose from the couch to straighten her short skirt and smooth her hair. No doubt, she was readying herself for her next appearance as a hooker.

And no matter how much he appreciated her

commitment to the job, he still hated the fact that she'd taken on such a dangerous assignment this time. He'd read the file on the missing women around town. Whoever was behind the suspected flesh trade quietly growing around Vegas, they were doing a damn good job of stealing women without a trace.

"Looks like we've got news," Simon warned her as he clicked open the e-mail with *positive ID* in the header.

On the other side of the room, Dorian went still.

"Tex is actually a Mississippi boy with one prior for soliciting a prostitute. His name is Matthew Hollins and he's a poker champ on tour with a group playing in Vegas for two weeks."

"Doesn't sound like the kind of guy exporting women to foreign hellholes." Dorian thumped her fist on the marble kitchen counter. "We need to get back out there and dig for more information before this weekend slips away. We don't want to miss a kidnapping because we're looking in the wrong direction."

"But this Matt could be a field soldier in a bigger operation. We could pick him up. Question him."

She shook her head, unsatisfied. "He's more use to us as our ticket into that party tomorrow night. I don't know about you, but I don't plan to settle for a few low-level arrests. When we nail the bastards, we're going to end this."

An ambitious goal. One he supported, but it wouldn't be easy. He wanted to refine their plans, to hammer out the best way to flush out their bigger targets.

Too bad Dorian was already on her way to the door.

"I'm going to see who else comes my way if I make a few laps around the casino. I'll be back in an hour."

"Wait." He rose from the computer, shutting the laptop.

The door closed behind her, leaving a yawning silence in her wake.

OBVIOUSLY SHE HADN'T thrown herself fully into her role last time, or she wouldn't have come up empty-handed for suspects. Dressed like she was, why wouldn't a black-market sex slave trader at least take a closer look at her?

Swinging her hips with every ounce of remembered feminine wile she never indulged, Dorian turned it up a notch, determined this weekend would yield the arrests this town needed.

As she turned into the main casino, a throng of

young guys passed her, their hands all clutching beers and plastic cups full of slot machine tokens. The cat calls were the deafening homage of the inebriated, bringing her attention from all over the casino floor.

Why hadn't she been able to tell Simon why this cover hurt so much for her? She couldn't deny she'd leaped at the chance to flee his suite, embarrassed by the past she hadn't come to terms with.

"Hey, beautiful." A soft masculine voice reached her ears from beside the roulette wheel, a vaguely foreign accent twisting the words into a musical sound.

She blinked to help her focus again, her gaze landing on an expensively dressed man who might have been European. His dark hair and darker eyes suggested Greek or Italian, but she was no expert on accents.

Forcing herself back into work mode, Dorian concentrated on her job. Approaching the man with a siren's walk and what she hoped passed for a seductive smile, she steeled herself against distracting emotions.

"Hi. Need some company?" Her heart slammed against her ribs, nervous and hoping she wasn't wasting valuable man-hours on some run-of-the-mill guy searching for a good time. She needed to find the key players, the power behind the throne.

Tex sure as hell wasn't the right man.

"I've been waiting for company." He set a drink down on top of a slot machine and stepped toward her, his intense stare starting to freak her out. "Let us go to my room."

"Don't you want to hear more about the full range of my services first?" She needed to stall a little longer, talk to him. She'd worry about how to extricate herself from a trip to his room later.

"Money is no issue." He wrapped an arm possessively around her waist. Gooseflesh born of revulsion mottled her skin. She was torn between the impulse to knee him in the groin and the need to wrest information from this scumbag.

The job won out.

"Are you from around here?" She sucked in her gut to buy herself an inch of freedom from his hand where it rested above her hip.

"No. I grew up in Cyprus but my business takes me around the globe. Do you like to travel?"

The international connection fit the profile for the group they'd been targeting. Dorian exclaimed over how much she loved the West Coast before turning the conversation back to him in the hope of figuring out if he could be one of the key figures in their case.

"But tell me all about you. Where do you travel most often?" She tried not to tense her fingers into a fist while her hand rested on his back as they walked the endless maze of casino that separated them from the hotel rooms.

"Indonesia. Singapore. Hong Kong. Where would you like me to take you?" He steered them past a long hallway full of Roman columns that led to the spa. A waitress wearing a short toga hurried by with a tray full of drinks.

"Me?" Her heart thumped all the louder at his offer. Could he be one of their guys? "I could never afford to travel to those exotic places. I've been saving my pennies for a road trip to Tahoe."

Better that she sound desperate if she wanted to make herself a target.

The man turned his head toward her and whispered in her ear.

"Then stick with me, love."

They arrived at the elevator banks just as a car chimed its arrival. They nearly ran right into Simon, looking harried and more than a little annoyed.

Dorian caught his eye for only a second before she risked a quick search over her shoulder for her companion. She couldn't afford to tip off her best lead yet that she wasn't what she seemed.

"Damn." Simon's voice loomed closer as she stepped into the car with her next would-be customer.

Simon was two steps behind them, smiling apologetically.

"Left my car keys in my room," he explained, checking his watch. "Looks like I'm going to be late after all."

Dorian didn't know whether to be grateful or worried that her partner for the weekend had decided to follow them, but there wasn't anything she could do about it. Would Simon be too quick to take chances and break cover at the first hint of danger? She was certain he wouldn't do that for any other officer. This case had him as off balance as her.

Focusing on her companion, she introduced herself.

"I'm Denise, by the way. Denise Rose."

"Anatole Konstantinou." He lowered his voice to keep their conversation intimate, but Dorian would bet money Simon overheard.

She just hoped Anatole's name wasn't as fake as hers. Then again, how many men gave out their real names to hookers?

"How long are you in town for, Anatole?" she whispered back, watching the numbers rise on the digital display as they went up to the penthouse level.

Simon had hit the button for one floor below the penthouse, no doubt to follow her more unobtrusively by way of the stairs. Assuming he didn't intervene before then with some he-man grandstanding. But he remained silent.

"As long as it takes to find the right travel companion." Anatole rubbed a finger over his upper lip as the elevator slowed for Simon's floor. Was the gesture a tell because he was lying?

Or would this guy truly try to coerce a hooker to travel abroad with him?

Simon exited the elevator and took a quick right. As soon as the doors closed behind him, Anatole hit another button three floors down.

"What are you doing?" Surprise shocked the breathy giggle right out of her voice.

"The man in here just now was a cop." He spat out the word as if it had an unpleasant taste. "I can spot them twenty yards away."

The possibility gave her shivers as he turned her in his arms to face him. Had he seen through her cover, as well?

"What do you care if he's a cop?" She smiled wickedly and splayed her hand against his shoulder to prevent him from leaning closer and closer to her. "Have you been very bad?"

The elevator sank and Dorian tried not to panic.

Sure she needed to get off the elevator before Anatole decided to get his money's worth right here in the privacy of a mirrored lift, but it wouldn't help anything if she started to sweat now.

"I hate cops," he confided, slipping her jacket off one shoulder to expose bare skin and cleavage.

Never had an elevator taken so long to reach its destination.

"Sorry, Anatole." She shrugged the jacket back over her shoulders. "I think we need to work out a few business details before we start getting naked."

The elevator chimed for the floor he'd pressed, but before the doors could open, Anatole hit the emergency button. Alarm blaring, the doors remained sealed shut.

Four floors away from where Simon expected her to be.

"I don't do quickies in the elevator." She itched to have her gun in hand, but if she drew a weapon now, her cover would be blown before she had accomplished anything on the case.

What had it been like for the women who were forced into servitude overseas? How would it feel to be trapped like this when there wasn't the mental reassurance of a concealed weapon in your purse?

"Doesn't it help in your line of work to have a sense of adventure?" He settled his hands on her waist and stepped closer, his groin brushing her hip and nudging his arousal sickeningly close to the juncture of her legs.

It didn't help that she'd worn a skirt that barely covered her. Dorian decided that was all she needed to call off the agreement in a believable way. No self-respecting working girl would let a man get away with so much.

"In my business, too much adventure can get you killed." She stepped backward out of his grip. "I think you've taken enough free feels, Mr. Konstantinou. I'd like to return to the casino floor."

Her cell phone started ringing then and she answered it in spite of her companion's lethal glare.

"Sorry I've been out of touch. I'll be back on the Abundance Thoroughfare in two minutes." She reached around Anatole to depress the emergency switch, leaving her cell phone connected so that Simon could overhear every word.

"Get the hell out of there, Dorian. Now." The gritty tension in Simon's voice surprised her.

The doors opened and she walked out of the elevator to hit the call button for a different lift, shooting the man behind her an apologetic glance to soothe his ego in case he was their man. It wouldn't be wise to burn bridges.

"Sorry, Anatole. Maybe another time?"

"You're making a mistake, Ms. Rose." Anatole's voice echoed in the hallway behind her, and she turned toward him. His eyes lingered on her, his still stance belying the anger that flashed across his handsome face. "There may come a day when you wish you had powerful allies in a dangerous business such as yours."

CHAPTER FOUR

THE DOORS CLOSED between Dorian and the man who called himself Anatole, taking him back to his penthouse suite, while another elevator arrived behind her. She turned to enter it and ran right into Simon.

"Where is he?" Simon closed his phone and put it in his pocket as he assessed the surroundings. "Are you okay?"

"Fine. But he guessed you were a cop." She tucked her phone back in her purse, right next to the service weapon she hadn't wanted to draw earlier. "My gut says that's our guy."

"How do you know?" He slid his hand over her hair in a gesture that was totally inappropriate for their working relationship and totally right at the same time.

She hadn't realized how tightly wound she'd been.

"He fits the profile of the ringleader we've

heard about, and he said that one day I'd wish I had powerful friends. His tone suggested to me he knew I'd be in trouble soon." Something about his demeanor seriously creeped her out and she'd never been a woman easily creeped. Anatole had meant to threaten her.

"Could have just been a little ego stroke to himself since you rejected him. Some guys think having money in the bank is a big power trip that makes them irresistible to women." Simon shuttled her into the elevator and hit the button for his suite.

"No." She knew what Simon was talking about but that didn't account for her gut impression. "I saw his face when he said it. He wanted to threaten me."

"Are you sure you're okay?" Simon tipped her chin up to look at him and only then, when her face was locked in the steadiness of his warm palm, did she realize she'd been shaking all over.

"I'm fine." She willed the trembling to stop. "I've handled murder scenes, Ramsey. You know I'm fine."

"None where you've had to tangle with potential murderers in a miniskirt with no backup in sight."

"You think the miniskirt makes any difference?" She wrenched away from him, unaccountably pissed off that she cared what this man thought about her in this outfit. "I could have taken that pig out wearing a thong if I needed to. Clothes don't define me."

She stomped off the elevator, her heels grinding into the carpet with each forceful step as she walked away from him.

CLEARLY, HE'D MADE A judgment error with the reference to her attire. Not the first today, now that he thought about it.

Simon stalked down the hall behind her, knowing something was seriously wrong for her to flip out over a miniskirt reference. Something was up with Dorian on this case and he intended to find out what.

As he rounded the last corner to his suite in the oval-shaped building, he spotted her leaning against the wall beside his door.

"You would have been a sight to behold in a thong." Simon slid the card in the lock, hoping she'd see the humor in the situation now that she'd had a minute to calm down.

To stop shaking.

"You'd make quite a sight yourself in a thong." Her voice sounded steadier now as she followed him into his room and closed the door behind her.

"Now that's a painful picture." He shuddered as he unfolded his computer screen and connected to a secure Web site.

She was quiet while he entered the information about Konstantinou along with a request from the hotel for a list of all the guests registered in a penthouse suite. There couldn't be many.

When he finished, his gaze tracked back to Dorian. She had kicked off her high heels and stood in the middle of the living area in her stocking feet. The curtains behind her were open, the neon signs from a casino across the street backlighting her in gaudy stripes of color.

"I'm a little touchy about this assignment," she said without prelude, her voice steady and strong.

"You never got around to telling me why this one had gotten under your skin." As soon as he'd finished trying to convince her that everyone gets too close to an investigation now and then, she'd bolted out the door to flush out new suspects.

"My mother turned tricks for a few years of my childhood. Five, actually."

She seemed to wait for that to sink into his head, but somehow, it didn't. It wouldn't. The pieces didn't fit.

"Are you trying to tell me—" He couldn't

reconcile this new revelation about Dorian with the woman he knew. Dorian was driven, focused, ambitious. And yeah, a little uptight. She defined professionalism. He'd figured she just put her guard up to keep her distance from all the guys she worked with.

But her need to keep her distance was probably rooted in something a hell of a lot darker than he'd ever guessed.

Damn.

"My mother was a prostitute." She confirmed what he hadn't been able to say. "She did it to keep a roof over our heads, but I never really forgave her for it because she died when I was still a stupid teenager. I hate that she left this world thinking I looked down on her for what she did, that I didn't appreciate her sacrifices."

The brittle hurt in her voice told him exactly how hard it was to admit what she perceived as a shortcoming in herself. He'd bet money she'd shared this information with almost no one. Something about the way she told him made him think this revelation was a first. Still…hadn't she at least shared it with her chief?

"Your commander must have known this would be a rough-as-hell assignment for you." Why had she been sent out on a job that would churn up a harrowing past? Those years her mother had been in the business had to have been hell.

"He doesn't know about it. My mother was harassed by cops a few times, but never arrested. After the first year or two, she took only the most upscale work through a legalized escort service. It kept her a little safer."

"I'm sure if you asked Captain Pearson to give the assignment to someone else—"

"And risk having to reveal a secret I've kept for this long? No thanks. Besides, as much as the job sucks, I like the idea of nailing the kind of creeps that harass women like my mom."

The fierce light in her eyes told him she wouldn't back down. And damned if he didn't admire that about her. He wanted to touch her. To offer her comfort of some kind. But she could be so prickly about stuff like that, and he'd never been much of a finesse guy.

"But this gig is already getting too personal." The extra risk she took today made more sense now. "I don't have to tell you that the cops who get too involved in a case are the first ones to make mistakes on the job."

Although who was he to talk? He'd gone a little insane when he realized she hadn't gotten off the elevator on the penthouse level earlier, his objectivity out the window where she was concerned. He'd already phoned hotel security to see if they could pick her up on any of the property's security cameras.

"I can't worry about that." She shook her head, silky dark hair grazing her cheek. "Ten years ago one of my mom's roommates disappeared, and we all assumed she'd been murdered by some overzealous client or a crazy on the street. But nobody ever turned up and the police never made any arrests."

"It's an at-risk population." He told her what she already knew, but he was at a loss how to make her situation any better. "That's why they're preyed on by groups like the one that's exporting sex slaves."

"About a year later, one of my mom's longterm clients came to her after a business trip to Korea and swore he'd seen the roommate in a bordello over there. He said she appeared strung out and high, but definitely the same woman. He tried to talk to her, but the owner booted him out of the place when he said he knew her."

"You think the same thing happened to her that is happening now to local women?" The idea of turning prisoners into junkies to keep them complacent certainly wasn't born in the twenty-first century.

"I do." She flipped idly through the pages of a room service menu while she spoke. "And something Konstantinou, or whatever his name is, said to me in the elevator made me realize that potential victims probably go willingly with their captors at first."

"What?" He tapped the menu. "And pick out what you want to eat. We can grab a bite while we research the guy more tonight."

"He offered to fly me to one of his international business destinations as a perk of our future relationship." She pointed out the sampler tray of grilled club sandwiches and then flipped to the directory of spa treatments at the back of the hotel guide. He had the feeling she wanted to break the intensity of a conversation that had to be tough for her.

"I'll bet that kind of invitation sounds mighty good to someone who hasn't had the chance to travel before."

"Even just having that much security for a couple of weeks sounds good to a woman who usually has a revolving door to her bedroom."

He picked up the phone to order in a couple of trays for a late dinner. Covering the mouthpiece with his hand, he said to Dorian, "You want me to order up a massage for you while I'm at it?"

Startled, she slammed the directory shut and straightened from the high island countertop.

"No. I'm not a fan of strangers touching me." She couldn't hide a shudder at the thought.

How much tougher had that made it for her to stomach the octopus hands of Tex and Konstantinou?

"I'm not a stranger." He didn't know why he felt compelled to point that out when she'd clearly had a rough day.

Hell, maybe it had been exactly *because* she'd had a rough day.

"Thanks, but I'll be fine." She folded her arms in a stance that normally meant a return to business, but with the low-cut corset on underneath her jacket, she merely put on a mouth-watering show.

"Do you really mean to blow me off all the times you say stuff like that, or is that just your autopilot response to any guy who flirts with you?" He'd chased her for months to no avail, never getting anywhere with her until that one night when she had seemed strangely ready to cut loose.

"You're asking *me* about my motives?" Shaking her head, she smiled that rare Dorian grin, the one that appeared only when she was finding humor in something no one else appreciated.

"Yeah. I am. What gives with the knee-jerk responses every time I've ever asked you to do anything with me?"

"Except for once."

"As I recall, you're the one who ultimately did the asking that night."

"And look how that turned out."

"Why *did* you ask me to go home with you that night?" He hadn't really thought about their one time together from that angle before since he'd been so caught up in his own guilt for walking away without even waking her up. "I was so bowled over by you after all the times you told me no that I didn't think to question my sudden turn of good fortune."

"But you're questioning it now?" She drummed her short fingernails on the marble island, her gaze focused on the heavy golden ring she wore on her right forefinger.

"Yes." Better he wised up now than later. "What made you walk across that bar to me a year ago?"

ROOM SERVICE DEMONSTRATED impeccable timing by choosing that moment to arrive with food for their late-night dinner. Dorian was grateful for the lightning-fast service for the high-roller suite, even though she'd lost her appetite the moment Simon had decided to revisit the past.

While Simon tipped the guy and removed the silver domes from the serving trays, Dorian tried to tell herself everything would be fine.

But she'd been fortunate Simon had never questioned her about her motives before now. She'd had a whole year to come to terms with what had happened in the days that led up to that one night together. How would he get a handle on finding out in one day?

Right in the middle of an investigation they were working together?

"Are you ready to eat or did you want to wait?" Simon's question made her realize the guy from room service was gone.

No more delays.

"I'll wait." She couldn't think about club sandwiches when she needed to clear the air. "Although I'll take the lemonade."

She swiped her drink off one of the trays and stole a sip. The moment reminded her about her accidental bout of drunkenness earlier in the day, and she felt compelled to relay the incident to Simon in lengthy detail to put off their current conversation.

And while he expressed shock and dismay in all the right places, he quickly steered them back to his real concern—after testing her lemonade for possible contamination.

"I'm getting the feeling I'm not going to particularly like your motives for going home with me that night, am I?" He rolled his shirtsleeve back, one crisp fold of fabric after another.

There was something inherently masculine in the movement, a slow unveiling of raw male power beneath the trappings of a gentleman. Her heart jumped in speed as she watched him from a few feet away, him spotlighted under the recessed lighting of the dining room, her in the dim living room.

She leaned against the back of the couch and set aside the lemonade.

"Bottom line, I wanted to be with you." It probably ranked as the most provocative statement she'd ever made to a man. But he deserved to know that basic truth before going into the rest of the story. "Despite the cool vibe I put out—and that's a habit I can't help because of issues I have with men in general—I definitely had the hots for you."

"Had." He repeated the word as if this was the most significant thing he could find in a loaded statement. "That's past tense?"

"Can we maybe deal with one thing at a time here?"

"Got it." He reached for his lemonade and took a long drink.

"But even though it had been a semi-well-established fact among my friends and coworkers that I suffered a small…affection…for you, I would have never approached you that night without some prodding."

"You're trying to tell me I owe it to cheap wine and the nudge of your girlfriends that you made your way across a crowded room to talk to me."

She wished she could leave it at that. But that wouldn't be totally honest of her, would it?

"Actually, you were part of a bet. I bet my friends I'd be the first woman in the Las Vegas Police Department to see you naked."

CHAPTER FIVE

"AND THIS WOULD offend me…how?" This was her big secret?

"You're not mad?" Her relief seemed genuine, the stiff set of her shoulders easing.

"Why would I be mad? A gorgeous woman sets out to seduce me? That's a fantasy for guys." He'd half hoped that she hid a secret more nefarious to balance out the fact that he'd left at dawn the next day and never called to clear things up with her.

"You have to admit, if a man did that to a woman—you know, made a bet with his friends that he'd get her into bed—a woman would think that was pretty raunchy."

"That's the difference between men and women. We're all pretty much game for being seduced." His gaze slid south along Dorian's admirable curves. "What I want to know is where are those friends of yours to coerce you into seducing me now?"

"They're both working undercover assignments around the city this weekend. But I don't think they'd be so quick to turn me loose on a man now. Last time they were mostly trying to help me forget about the perp I shot the week before."

Simon set down his lemonade glass, figuring the clinking ice cubes must have interfered with his hearing.

"Run that by me again?"

She twisted the gold ring around her index finger.

"I'd shot my first suspect during an arrest gone bad the week before our night together. The guy pulled a gun before we got the cuffs on him in a suspected assault charge. I'd been really torn up about it because they didn't expect the guy to live, but then we got some additional evidence in our case that he'd raped a mother of two before killing her." She shook her head hard, as if she could physically shake off unpleasant memories.

Simon didn't remember walking over to her, but he was suddenly right in front of her, folding her into his arms.

"You did the right thing."

"I know." She nodded against his shoulder even as he felt a warm tear soak through his shirt. "But I'd found out that morning that the guy was going to pull through after all and I had this moment of—it's awful to say—but just this wrenching disappointment that I'd somehow let the woman down. And while I stifled the reaction, I knew it had been there and it made me feel like a monster. Like I was no better than the creep I shot."

"You know better now, right?" He stroked her hair while she kept her face buried against his shoulder. "Internal Affairs wouldn't have cleared you if you were a monster. They wouldn't have you working cases like this one if they thought you posed a threat. But you didn't shoot him because you thought he raped a woman. You took him down because he defied the authority of a cop and resisted arrest. If you hadn't acted, you would have been knowingly unleashing a criminal with no respect for the law onto the streets."

"I didn't have to think such bloodthirsty thoughts."

"Every cop in the world has had those thoughts, babe, or they wouldn't be human. No father could arrest a child molester without wanting to wreak stark, personal vengeance right then and there. But good cops don't act on those thoughts, they just make the arrest and hope like hell the justice system works."

Here, at least, was the real reason she'd hit on him that night. It didn't have a damn thing to do with a bet and had everything to do with being caught in an emotional nightmare. Today he was seeing facets of Dorian he'd never even suspected. And hell, underneath it all she'd admitted to liking him at one time.

That in itself blew him away.

"Sorry to unload all of this on you when we have a million other things to think about." She straightened, a deep breath bracing those stubborn shoulders of hers all over again.

"We don't, though. From what I can tell now, it's a waiting game." He couldn't make himself let go of her just yet, his hands curving around her shoulders to hold her there another minute. "We find out what we can on Konstantinou and wait for Tex's party to see if his high-powered friends are as dangerous as we think they might be."

"Are you suggesting we don't have anything to do until tomorrow?" She didn't shake loose of his touch, but she didn't exactly melt in his arms, either. "That seems like too much time to fill with my life saga. We've been back in each other's company for less than twenty-four hours, and I've already told you all my worst stories."

He smoothed his fingertips across the tops of

her shoulders, remembering exactly what she felt like without her jacket on. Without anything on. His awareness of her—already hyper-attuned—couldn't miss the way her breath caught when he touched her.

"Want me to brainstorm ways to fill the time?" His top three all involved peeling Dorian's clothes off, but he didn't share that with her for fear of scaring her away.

"I could start by apologizing for coming on to you when I didn't have my head on straight. While it was convenient and relieved me of a certain amount of guilt that you left first that morning, I guess there's a good chance I might have done the same thing if I'd opened my eyes before you."

Her words stung just a little, but they were damn well soothed by the fact that he had his hands on her, remembering every curve and nuance of her softly scented skin.

"Even though you didn't have the excuse of being undercover like me?"

"I was in the middle of a moral crisis." She shrugged, her shoulder rising beneath his palm. "That's enough of an excuse."

"Interesting." He slid his hands closer to her neck, dipping slightly beneath her jacket to massage her shoulders without the extra layer of clothing. "Ever wonder why you need the excuse of a crisis to be with me? To be with any man?"

SHE MIGHT HAVE BEEN more offended by his words if her skin hadn't been on fire from his touch.

Dorian struggled for the right response to his question—denial or an argument? But the longer she allowed Simon's incredible hands to work her over, to generate heat and hunger inside her, the more she realized she had no good reason.

Only excuses.

"Sex comes with a lot of mental baggage when your mom's a…um…professional." She'd known it, but she'd never admitted it out loud. Maybe she hadn't even really admitted it to herself.

Putting the simple truth out there relieved her somehow, clearing the way for a solution or at least a plan of action.

His thumbs dipped beneath the bra straps of her corset, unleashing an electric current of heat even though his hands remained on the tops of her shoulders.

"I've heard tossing baggage out the window every now and then can be very freeing."

"Is that right?"

"You could decide to be with me just because

you're dying to have me and not because any life explosion has tipped you sideways."

She couldn't answer while she held her breath, waiting for his thumbs to work their way down a little farther. But he stilled, halting his progress for a few interminable seconds until she understood she had to make a decision.

Did she want Simon now, when she couldn't write off her response to him as an adrenaline by-product of the job? Saying yes to him now would mean admitting a deeper attraction than she'd ever owned up to before.

Her body urged her to acknowledge it. Fulfill it. Her spine arched subtly toward his touch in silent admission of everything she wanted.

"Well?" he pressed, his voice taking on a smoky, bedroom quality she wanted breathed all over her skin.

"I—" Confessing a weakness for Simon made her vulnerable to him. To this. But dear God, who would she be kidding if she denied it? "I want you."

Decision made, her knees went weak beneath her, making her sway toward him. A force stronger than gravity seemed to draw her there, urging her closer to him.

Their mouths met in a melting moment that

turned her whole body liquid. She sighed her pleasure, parting her lips to the seductive stroke of his tongue between her teeth.

Heat engulfed her, intensifying everything she felt for him. It had been a whole year since she'd kissed a man, touched a man. No, not just any man. *Simon.*

Powerful feelings wound up with toe-curling responses, making it difficult for her to tell where one ended and the other began. She'd wanted him for so long before she'd slept with him last time. He'd been patient with her rebuffs, waiting for her to see him as more than just some guy who liked to flirt with her.

Then she'd dragged him back home with her in a night of professional crisis. Sabotaging a relationship purposely?

"Simon?" She broke off the kiss, panicked at the thought.

He blinked back at her, eyes as passion-dazed as she knew hers must be.

"Please say you're not bailing on me now." He twined one of the laces from her corset around his finger and tugged gently. "I wanted to see you come all undone for me tonight."

"We have to promise to still be in this bed in the morning." She didn't know if that sounded like the plea of an insecure woman, but she understood they needed to talk. "I'm asking that of myself as much as you or we shouldn't go through with this."

"I promise I won't let you out of bed until after sunrise." He pulled the lace harder, untying the ribbon from its bow in the valley of her cleavage and ignoring all the pesky hooks at her back that she'd worked hard to fasten. Why did she have to fight so hard to accomplish things that came so easily to other people? "What about you, Dorian? Are you going to do your best to keep me here all night?"

The corset loosened its hold on her breasts and ribs, sliding open to her waist before hitching on her hips.

She appreciated his easy acceptance of her terms, his ability to turn her request into a sensual challenge. If any man could help her see the lighter side of sex, he could. And that sounded so enticing tonight, when her world wanted to crash in on her from all sides.

"Are you kidding?" She helped him undo the last of the lacing that allowed the corset to skim all the way to the floor. "I've been without for a whole year. I'm prepared to make sure you can hardly move in the morning, let alone walk away."

Stepping out of the corset, she reached for the waistband of her skirt. She had no idea if she could make good on her threat, but it would be fun to try. Just watching Simon's eyes zero in on her hand at her waist sent a thrill through her clear down to her toes.

"Let me." He reached for the zipper to unfasten her skirt.

Fingertips brushing her skin, he worked the hooks and lowered the tab, revealing the red panties that matched the corset. She hadn't planned on anyone seeing that part of her costume, but since the whole get-up came as a set, she'd figured the full working-girl regalia would help ground her in the cover. Hearing Simon's ragged intake of breath now as he eased her skirt off to reveal the garter belt and panties was a delectable bonus.

"You're getting ahead of me," she whispered, unfastening the buttons on his shirt in a sudden urge to get him naked. "Let me catch up."

Was he as impressive as she remembered? They'd only been together that one night and her perceptions had been ever so slightly colored by alcohol. Could he possibly be as well built as she made him in her daydreams?

"Take your time." He traced the lace on her

garter belt with his finger, curving around her hip and then angling in toward her belly. "I could look at you all night."

Tugging his shirttails free of his pants, she undid the last of the buttons and pushed the shirt off his shoulders. *Umm.* If his chest was anything to judge by, this man would live up to every one of her memories.

She undid his belt buckle, her fingers grazing the hard heat of him through his trousers. Her heart rate kicked up as she tugged the leather out of the belt loops and tossed it aside.

Before she could unfasten his fly he lifted her off her feet to kiss her, pressing her body to his. Her bare breasts grazed his chest. She whimpered with hunger at the feel of him when he aligned their hips for one heart-stopping minute. She broke free of the kiss, desperate to make her wishes known.

"I want you to do more than look." Her words tripped over her ragged breaths, her whole body tingling with need. Her head buzzed with urgency as if she had a chorus of rising drumbeats pounding inside her brain.

"By all means, Dor, tell me everything you want and that's exactly what I'm going to give you." His hands were molded to her backside, holding her against him and he wriggled his fingers now for emphasis.

Heat shot through her, inspiring her to spell out her wishes while she had the chance.

"I want your hands all over me. I want us both naked. I want to be under you, over you and all around you. Then I want you to take me on the dining table, the sofa and the bed. Then maybe against the balcony doors. Then on the balcony with the lights of the Strip reflecting all over us." She could think of ten other ways she wanted him. "Or else scratch all that and do whatever you will with me as long as you're inside me."

For one pulse-pounding moment she thought maybe she'd rendered Agent Type A speechless. But he recovered in the next second, whipping around to head toward the dining room.

"That has to be the hottest to do list any woman has ever given a man." He wrapped her legs around his waist to carry her in a way that brought the neediest part of her in sweetly pleasurable contact with the hardest part of him. "Since the dining table is closest, it looks like I'm going to make a feast of you first."

CHAPTER SIX

SIMON REMEMBERED EXACTLY how hot he'd been for Dorian the last time they'd fallen into bed together. The sex had been as phenomenal as he'd ever imagined and better.

But this time was different.

He settled her on the long, oval-shaped table centered underneath a crystal chandelier, the polished hardwood surface gleaming under the low setting of the overhead lighting. This time his heart had been called into the act so sharply he'd be an idiot not to notice. Her plea for sex all over the hotel suite might seem like a normal, healthy drive for a red-blooded woman, but he knew that carnal request hadn't come easily for Dorian. Her upbringing had made her a conservative woman—a woman who dressed in gray flannel and pastel silks, a woman who took her job seriously because she'd made it the focal point of her life. She'd never dated anyone on the force that he knew of, and he'd kept close tabs on her for nearly two years now.

For her to trust him this way seemed all the more significant since she usually kept a tight rein on herself.

"Don't move," he cautioned her, wanting everything to be perfect for her. He backed away a step to memorize every facet of her, her cheeks flushed and wild dark hair curling against her jaw, then he sprinted back to a cabinet of linens in the hallway. Bringing a blanket back with him he snapped the cotton throw with his wrists to billow behind her and then wrapped it around her like a cape.

She smiled, her red lips curving upward to reveal straight white teeth. "I'm a big girl, Agent Ramsey. You don't have to protect me."

"If I'm going to fulfill all those wishes of yours I have a vested interest in making sure I don't give you rug burn. Or table burn in this case." He unfastened his pants, freeing him from a confinement he couldn't handle any longer.

She caught him in her hands, running her fingers up the length of him through his boxers. His eyes were crossing before his trousers hit the floor. Her thighs—bare except for the hint of stocking still strapped to her legs—hugged his, her ankles lodged behind his knees to draw him close.

"Promises, promises," she taunted him, rubbing her breasts against his bare chest as she leaned closer. "Where is all this fierce activity that could give me table burn?"

She circled the tip of him with one finger before yanking his boxers down and off. She eyed him with open longing and it was all he could do not to plant himself deep inside her right that second. Her red mouth matched the crimson of her lace panties still clinging to her hips by fragile ribbons tied in tiny bows.

"I'm sorry I've had to make you wait," he whispered in her ear, tipping her back against the table to lie down. "But I promise it's for your own good. Remember I told you there would be feasting first?"

He untied the skinny laces at her hips and pulled her panties off, baring her to him. She arched her back, hips restless as he made his way down her body to taste her.

Her breath hissed between her teeth as he kissed her intimately. Another time he might have lingered to take off her garters and press kisses up the inside of her thigh, but he couldn't afford that kind of side detour now, tempting though it might be. He teetered close to the edge himself after going without her for so many months, but he was determined she'd cross that line first. And thanks to inside information about what she liked, he happened to know this would take Dorian to that sensual high the fastest.

Her breathing came quicker as she cried out a string of sweet nonsense, her hips lifting to meet his mouth. He pressed harder, drawing on the swollen center of her until her thighs clenched helplessly around his shoulders and she shouted with the first waves of her orgasm. He gave no quarter, sliding his finger inside her to tease every last delicate spasm from her.

When her cries turned to pleas for more he released her, wrenching a condom from his pants pocket before he stretched out over top of her. She covered his face in kisses as she tried to sit up, her fingers tugging the packet out of his hands to take over the task herself.

By now he had no choice but to let her. He was teetering so close that any lingering stroke of her hands could probably send him hurtling into endless completion, so he concentrated all his energy on simply surviving her touches.

The scent of her clung to his skin, making him crazy. Her thighs clenched his, drawing him to her even while she kept him at arm's length to roll the condom down him. Her fingers trembled with the aftershocks of the sexual high she'd reached, and he promised himself it wouldn't be the last time he had her quivering like that.

"I can't wait to be inside you." He told her the bare truth, his hunger for her so raw and basic that he couldn't imagine ever looking at her without wanting her again.

The tenderness in her eyes slugged him hard as she aligned their bodies and he knew he'd never wanted to possess a woman so completely. Then her eyes slid closed and—finally, at last, thank you—he eased himself between her thighs.

Her head tipped back, arching her breasts high and within tasting distance from his mouth. He watched his hands cover them, shape them, mold them toward his mouth, the tan of his skin a sharp contrast to the paler color of her here, even with her golden skin tone. He nipped and sucked, pinching her gently between his fingers as he drove deeper inside her.

His thighs hit the table and he dragged her body back to the edge of the table, closer to him. Her eyes fluttered open at the movement, her gaze locked with his.

Something passed between them—a look, a feeling, a moment of connection—and Simon committed himself to her without hesitation. He slid his arms around her waist, drawing her up to sit on the table as he found the rhythm that would work for both of them. Her ankles locked around his waist as she squeezed him with her inner muscles and then all was lost.

Heat rushed through him at light speed, erasing anything but desire for Dorian. The force of his climax damn near brought him off his feet, the reverberations blasting through his whole body. He gathered her to him, powerless to communicate what he felt for her any other way. But maybe that's because he didn't fully comprehend it himself.

He'd never needed anyone before, his life as an FBI agent perfectly suited to a loner. But Dorian had snuck under his radar and become a vital part of him.

The thought scared him even before the sweat had a chance to dry off his skin.

In the past, he would have thought a night of nonstop sex might cure a growing attachment he felt for a woman, since time spent together sometimes served to highlight a couple's differences. With Dorian he knew that wouldn't be the case. And although he looked forward to delivering every sensual promise he'd made to her, he had the feeling he would be sticking by her side for more than just tomorrow.

DORIAN BLINKED HER WAY through sleep the next morning to hear Simon's voice talking in low and urgent tones.

The sound brought back a wealth of memories from the night before that had her smiling before her eyes even opened. Simon whispering darkly erotic suggestions in her ear while he teased her to completion out on the balcony. Simon shouting his own release in the shower after she'd poured champagne down his shaft to celebrate his commendable staying power after their fifth go-round. She now knew room service would bring condoms to the high-roller suites upon request.

She loved Las Vegas.

The sentiment surprised her suddenly as she realized what a departure last night had been for her. She'd always been so cautious with her sexuality, not sharing herself with anyone unless…it meant something special.

She pried her eyes fully open to find sunlight spilling over her naked body swathed in a sheet like the toga-wearing figures in frescoes all around them. Simon and all his unorthodox ways had become important to her almost without her realizing it, her feelings for him so wrapped up in hurt about that night a year ago that she hadn't questioned what might be lying beneath her embarrassment at being walked out on. Last night, apparently, she'd discovered her emotions went deeper than that or she would have never given herself so completely to Simon.

Had she even considered how difficult it might be to have a relationship with a man who didn't believe in following a game plan and liked to shoot from the hip? Tension knotted at the base of her spine as she realized they hadn't even finished their job together. Would she be able to work with a man who'd seen her with her guard completely down?

"But you're sure this guy knows Konstantinou?"

Simon's voice picked up volume in the other room, his words all the more meaningful since he was clearly discussing their case.

She wrapped the sheet more tightly around her and slid off the bed, heading for the suite's living area.

"I can't go to my deputy director with a bunch of hearsay. And, hell, I won't even get the casino's help on this one if there's a basketball star involved. You know how much status professional athletes bring to this city?" Simon sat on the arm of the sofa with his cell phone cradled against his shoulder while he worked on his laptop.

He'd dressed already, his white dress shirt unbuttoned to the waist, his khakis pressed and pleated. He flashed Dorian a brief smile as he spotted her, his gaze sliding south to take in her body wrapped in a bed sheet.

"I know." He shook his head at whatever the party on the other end of the phone was saying. "I know. And I appreciate this much. Thanks, bud."

Disconnecting the call, he set down his laptop and met her in the middle of the living room.

"Did you find out anything?" She didn't know the protocol for mingling work and pleasure, but right now she had to know what was happening with their case.

"Nothing concrete." He bent to brush his lips over hers. "Good morning."

She smiled. Possibly she blushed. Just the scent of him had her imagining what the day might be like if they had more time.

They didn't, of course. Time for the real world to return with a vengeance.

"Morning." She dropped into a low leather chaise across from the sofa. "What do you mean 'nothing concrete'? I heard you talking about Konstantinou."

"I asked an informant friend to see what he came up with on this guy and his sources say Anatole is linked to some heavy-hitter sports stars, including a basketball player who hits Vegas often and put a private helicopter at Konstantinou's disposal this week."

"Meaning he's got a great vehicle to transport out his women if he's our guy." She knew the neighboring hotel had a helipad. Would Konstantinou try to use it as an escape after the party tonight? Or were they looking at the wrong man altogether?

"If he's our guy." He spoke her thoughts aloud as he retrieved his laptop. "I don't know how much backing we'll get from your department, let alone the hotel, without concrete evidence."

"We'll get police backup outside the party tonight, since we had evidence going into the weekend that significant black-market players would be congregating at the Pompeii. My chief backs the sting." She wouldn't let Pearson down after all the ways he'd supported her in the weeks following last year's shooting. "But you've worked in this city long enough to know we're not going to be able to shut down a helipad or question a professional athlete without tons of just cause. Vegas is too dependent on celebrity money and celebrity visibility."

"Right." He turned the laptop monitor toward her so she could see what he'd been working on. A diagram of the Pompeii Hotel and Casino filled the screen. "That means we've got to be all the more vigilant about setting up our sting tonight. This is the penthouse suite where we're slated to meet—"

He paused midsentence, thumb pressed to the screen, as he turned toward her.

"What?"

"I can't— That is, it would help if you'd put clothes on." He kept his gaze rigidly on her face, but that didn't stop her body from becoming ultra-aware of him. Her skin tingled beneath the sheet.

"Good idea." She couldn't make tracks to the bedroom fast enough, grateful she'd moved a bag down here the day before. She didn't have her outfit for the party tonight, but she had a T-shirt and shorts to tide her over until then.

"Dorian?" He called to her before she reached the bedroom.

"Yeah?" She gripped the sheet to her breasts, not daring to turn all the way around—her pulse quickening and her body humming in anticipation. They needed to think about work, not about getting naked again.

"I hope you'll wear that sheet for me again sometime after we're done nailing these bastards." The heat in his gaze was tempered with a sincerity she couldn't help but recognize.

Her heart turned over inside her, temporarily robbing her of speech. Did he honestly want to make an effort with her? To see her again when their lives were sorted out and danger didn't dog their heels?

Nodding, she tried not to trip over her feet—and a tangible hopefulness—as she went to dress. Simon's Wildcard days might not be over, but maybe this case that had propelled her deep into the emotional terrain of her past would teach her some understanding for the man who pushed his career to the edge. If only they could make it through this one case, which meant so much to her—maybe then they could explore the possibility of a future.

SIMON COULDN'T SHAKE the fear of something going wrong that night, as he knotted his necktie on the way up the elevator to Dorian's room.

If it was just him at stake in the operation, he wouldn't care. He trusted his survival instincts and—to a certain extent—he'd always thrived on adrenaline. But tonight Dorian would be in the riskiest position. And although she'd probably be offended to know he was worried about her, he couldn't shake the impending sense of disaster that had hounded him ever since he'd opened his eyes this morning.

Not that he'd admitted as much to Dorian.

The elevator chimed as it stopped on her floor an hour before the party was supposed to start. He knew the LVMPD would be getting into their positions around the penthouse floor to make sure the party was well monitored for security, but he couldn't check out the preparations personally while under-cover. Dorian ran a by-the-book mission and she wouldn't appreciate his bending the rules to ease his mind, but the end result was that he felt restless. Edgy.

Damn.

Dorian's door flew open before he knocked, throwing him further off his game.

"Hi, baby." She smiled with a siren's calculated seduction. "I've been waiting for you."

He recognized her call-girl tone that she'd probably trotted out to perpetuate their cover. The knowledge that her act was fake didn't diminish his automatic response to her one bit.

Blood sizzled in his veins as her gaze roamed over his whole body. Her hair was damp from a shower and a short satin robe clung to her curves. The scent of soap wafted off her skin.

He followed that scent like a hound, crossing into her room on blind instinct. Reaching for her, he told himself he was only playing out his role the same way she played hers, in case anyone was watching them. The fact that his role involved touching her was a bonus.

He wrapped his arms around her waist and kissed her, his body responding instantly to hers in the insubstantial robe. And hot damn but she was naked underneath it.

The door to her room shut behind him and he bracketed her hips with his hands as he tasted her. He needed this connection with her before tonight so he could ease some of the sexual hunger....

"Simon."

His name echoed in his ears and it took him a second to realize she'd leaned back and away from him.

"What?" Releasing her instantly, he tried not to notice the way her breasts pressed against the confines of her robe.

"Working girls don't kiss with open mouths. You know that." Her eyebrows pinched together in a worried frown. "Anyone watching might think—" She shrugged.

"You're right." He took a step back, realizing his attraction to her had clouded his professional judgment. "Sorry."

"Did you see anyone in the hall?" The wrinkle between her eyes hadn't quite disappeared.

"No. Why? Do you think someone's been following you?" The sense of impending danger returned and he wondered if Dorian's cop radar twitched as much as his.

"Matt Gaines—Tex—called me earlier to make sure I would be at the party tonight. He kept up the good-old-boy act, but it sounded a little more forced. I wondered if someone was pressuring him to produce a certain number of women for this gig."

She wrapped her arms around herself, a vulnerable gesture he'd never seen from her in a work environment before. She'd always been so tough, so controlled. He hated that she'd taken on a sting operation that hit so close to home.

"We're going to catch these bastards, Dor." He traced her jawline with his fingers, careful not to indulge touches that might lead to an encounter they wouldn't be able to walk away from.

"Damn straight we will," she agreed, her gaze meeting his with an intensity he hadn't expected. "If we stick to the plan and don't throw each other any surprises, we'll make sure no more women disappear from Vegas."

His hand stilled on her cheek as he recognized her subtle way of laying down ground rules.

"I know we don't work the same way—"

"We can for one night, can't we?" She laid her

hands on his chest, stepping farther into his reach when he was trying like hell to disconnect from his hunger for her.

"Your safety is too important for me to promise this is going to happen the way you want it to. I can't go into a tense cover with my hands tied behind my back."

Her touch fell away from him.

"And you think that's what I'm doing? Tying you down?"

The phrase took on new meaning—a meaning he hadn't meant to imply. Had he?

"I can work as a team." He just hadn't found many opportunities to prove it. "But I happen to know that my ability to improvise in situations has propelled me out of a lot of hairy moments."

"I can't work when I don't know what could come out of your mouth next."

That's what it boiled down to. Dorian couldn't predict his next move and she hated that. Well, damned if he could predict what happened next, either.

CHAPTER SEVEN

"WHAT DO YOU THINK of these guys?" A young woman named Evangeline leaned close to Dorian a half hour into the party on the penthouse floor, her voice raised to be heard above the throbbing dance music. "Are they for real or are they just full of themselves and a weekend of big gambling wins?"

Dorian took the question seriously as she sipped her ginger ale with lime from a martini glass and hoped the private bartender who'd given it to her wouldn't sell her out for refusing alcohol. Most of the thirty-some attendees were already ordering booze by the bottle, the atmosphere only a shade more upscale than the VIP lounge of a strip club. Most of the twenty-one women in attendance wore clothes with a seriously provocative attitude from backless sheaths to plunging necklines and thigh-high slits that showed off generous amounts of leg. One woman in the center of the dance floor playfully stripped off her friend's blouse, the two of them working their attributes for all they were worth.

Clearly, some of the guests had bought into Matt Gaines's promises of unlimited income opportunities. She'd found out by talking to a handful of the women that Matt had invited most of them, but Anatole Konstantinou and another man had invited a few others. Dorian grew more and more certain that Matt and the other man worked on commission while Konstantinou was the top guy behind the prostitute disappearances.

"I don't know. They've got enough cash for a major bash, though." Dorian hoped no one expected her to dance like the women cavorting around the temporary flooring laid around the raised hot tub. First of all, she lacked the coordination to hump a dance pole. Second, her affinity with Murphy's Law meant someone would splash water from the tub on the parquet, and she'd end up sprawled on her butt in the most expensive sequined dress she'd ever worn. She was pretty sure the department would bill her if she ruined the outfit because of poorly executed booty-shaking.

"I'm sure they have the cash to pay for whatever they like," Evangeline agreed, eyes flitting over to where Anatole Konstantinou sat in heated conversation with Matt and two other men who seemed to be offering security to the party.

Off to one side of the group, Dorian noticed Simon lingering by the champagne fountain. No doubt he was trying to overhear what was being said.

When Dorian didn't respond, Evangeline continued.

"But will they be decent guys who uphold their end of the deal? Something about Konstantinou seems sort of cold, you know?"

Did she ever. Dorian wished she could tell all the women present to run like hell and not look back, but that wouldn't help solve the core problem, and it wouldn't facilitate the convictions they needed to keep them safe in the future.

"Do you work alone?" Dorian asked, wondering how long it would be before the party hosts would get around to making their move. The exits to the hotel were being watched to prevent anyone from leaving the party with one of these women, but Dorian could think of a million ways a subtle operator could elude the police trying to monitor a casino with thousands of people walking in and out every night.

"Yes. I have a young daughter at home so I can't afford to take any chances with roommates who aren't cautious. My baby is my whole life so I keep my home off-limits." Evangeline popped open a locket behind her heart-shaped watch to show Dorian a gorgeous little girl with yellow ribbons around brown pigtails.

The warmth in the young woman's voice socked Dorian in the chest along with a peculiar sense of connection. She could have been talking to her own mother twenty years ago, because that's exactly the kind of thing Candy would have said about her own home life. About her own daughter. But it was different to hear the words from her mother as a kid than to hear the words from someone Dorian's age. The love in Evangeline's voice couldn't be mistaken.

"She's beautiful," Dorian said finally, realizing she'd been staring into the little girl's face like a ghost from the past. "You must be very proud."

Just then Matt took the microphone away from the deejay and turned down the record. He jumped onto the dance floor right between the half-naked women.

"Attention, everyone, thank you for coming and welcome to Anatole's temporary palace of delights. There's more fun to be had at our subterranean lair. Just follow the champagne tray down the private elevator, and we'll lead you to stage two of our shindig. See you downstairs."

Stage two?

Dorian's skin chilled at the change of venue, never a good sign in criminal behavior. It took a supreme effort of will to look at Simon with no more than a vacuous giggle and a toss of her hair. Was the party moving because their suspects were wise to being watched? Or did Anatole and friends simply want to make abducting their next victim that much harder to trace?

From his position next to Anatole, Simon winked at Dorian while—interestingly—Anatole seemed to watch the exchange carefully. Did he think it suspicious that Simon was Dorian's pimp and had pretended not to know her yesterday in the elevator?

Brushing off the fear, she told herself that kind of protectiveness—riding up in the elevator with them—was typical of a pimp. Still, Anatole's obvious interest in them made her uneasy. Would he discount Dorian as a possible target for abduction if he thought Simon might come after him for his share of the cut?

Or would Anatole have Simon hurt—or worse— to eliminate any threat?

"Looks like not everyone's moving on to stage two," Evangeline observed as she peered over her shoulder.

The dancers of the impromptu striptease were being escorted into another part of the suite along with a handful of other women. Even without glancing across the room at Simon she could sense his tension at the scenario. No doubt he was thinking the same thing as her. What if it was the other group of women who'd been pegged for potential abduction, and Dorian couldn't be there to oversee what happened?

Nerves jangling uneasily inside her, Dorian forced herself to keep pace with Evangeline as they walked toward the private elevator that wouldn't be easily detected by the police backup who were watching the exits of the building and the penthouse floor in particular. Use of the elevator might not raise the red flag it should if trips were kept to a minimum and the noise of a party continued inside the hotel rooms. And since the penthouse elevators were operated with private keys, the access would be limited.

"I guess we're the lucky ones," Dorian murmured, wishing she could have worn a weapon within closer reach than the small pistol strapped on the inside of her thigh. She felt claustrophobic as ten guests crowded into one elevator, a feeling that increased when she realized Simon wouldn't make it into the same lift as her. The rowdy group sang and laughed and drank as they introduced themselves on the way down. Down. Down.

Where the hell were they going? The man in charge of the elevator keypad had used a key to open an access box that seemed like the type of thing only hotel staff should be able to use. Was a hotel staffer taking the group to a level that would be off-limits to the public? She hoped Simon had a way to contact their backup and alert them to the location change, because cell phone contact would be impossible if they were really headed below street level, like Dorian suspected.

Damn.

They needed more backup. More manpower if they wanted to keep all the women here safe.

But she had Simon. The wildcard fed who didn't stick to a plan but somehow got the job done anyway. And since her plan for this sting was going to hell in a hurry, maybe she'd be better off following the lead of a man who specialized in creative problem solving and bullshitting—that is, improvising his way through sticky situations.

Because as the elevator doors swished open on a gray, dark floor, Dorian suspected their trouble had only just begun. The party crowd spilled into the echoing basement space that appeared more like a food warehouse than a scene for festivities.

This was definitely not a public-access area. It looked like the overflow storage space for the kitchens, judging by the crates of canned goods lining one wall.

To make matters worse, the two buff young male escorts who greeted them each carried a machine gun strapped over his shoulder.

"THIS IS WHERE WE PART, Mr. Rainier." Anatole Konstantinou called Simon by his undercover name, but his polite tone didn't disguise the malice in the man's eyes.

Simon had been separated from Dorian by an elevator ride and who knew how many floors, and now Konstantinou wanted him to walk away? Not on his life. And if Simon had to call upon a few unorthodox tricks to get his way, he damn well would. He'd worry about the lecture from Dorian after. Her life was more important than running the operation by some rule book.

"I thought we were friends?" Simon did his best amiable-drunk-guy routine. "Come on. The night's still young and you're hoarding all the hottest chicks to yourself? Where's your sense of fair play?"

Anatole didn't respond, but his eyes cut over to a couple of his goons who seemed to be charged with making Konstantinou's every wish come true.

"I've got it," Simon continued, pretending to be oblivious to how much he was pissing off his host. "This is Vegas, right? How about a little friendly wager on the girls? Double or nothing? I've had my eye on the brunette hanging with Denise all night." Simon remembered Anatole only knew Dorian by her hooker name, Denise. "Ten thousand says I take her home with me and I get Denise back, too."

Anatole's eyes narrowed.

"What? You think I don't know you're trying to tie her up for yourself? You've had a hard-on for her all weekend. If I lose, she's all yours. If I win, I keep her and I get her friend, too. We put the ten thousand on the table just to keep things interesting."

Simon kept the elevator doors in his peripheral vision, since he'd have to sprint for it while trying to ward off the armed lackeys if Anatole didn't go for the bet. Simon's cover would be blown, but it didn't matter if Dorian was at risk. He could sense the time to make their arrests was fast approaching.

The mood in the room turned tense for a long moment until Anatole burst out in a short bark of laughter.

"Very well, Rainier." He gestured toward the elevator, the invitation Simon had been waiting for. "If you're willing to have my man hold your money."

Simon took the open path to the elevator, unwilling to risk Anatole's changing his mind. Only after he was safely inside the cabin with Konstantinou and two guards did Simon grin.

"Was I born yesterday?" Simon flashed his mark like it was no big deal, grateful the casino had staked the efforts this weekend so he could back up his words. "I'll give my mark to Denise's friend to hold. Deal?"

Behind the facade of his living-on-the edge cover persona, Simon made plans for his next move. Would he play out the game as promised? Or would he need to act as soon as the elevator doors opened? A lot depended on how much more evidence they needed for the intended crime and, more importantly, what condition Dorian was in wherever they'd taken her. If they'd hurt or drugged her, all bets were off and the D.A. would have to go after Konstantinou and friends with whatever evidence they'd already seen. But if Dorian wasn't hurt and didn't seem inclined to break cover yet, he'd wait on her cue.

He just hoped she didn't wait too long. Sometimes being too cautious caused more heartache in the long run. Witness their rocky relationship. As the elevator chimed on arrival, he promised himself he wouldn't wait around any longer for her to see they belonged together. As soon as they made some arrests tonight, he'd take Dorian someplace private and tell her as much.

"After you, Rainier," Konstantinou offered up from beside him in the elevator car.

The bowels of the Pompeii Hotel and Casino building were dimly lit and smelled like industrial laundry. The service elevator must hit this floor for access to the washer-and-dryer facilities or room service options since boxes of food goods divided the space into mazelike tunnels.

Simon strolled out of the lift with easy movements even though he was tense as hell inside. There was no music, no bar, no hint of a party here. Where was Dorian?

He spent precious seconds waiting for his eyes to adjust to the light.

"Damn, Konstantinou. How the hell do you deal cards in the dark? Or will you just trust me when I say I've got a full house?" Simon used the lack of light to pull a concealed 9mm from his waist.

"I'm afraid I've changed my mind on the terms

of our wager, friend." Konstantinou's voice echoed in the barren stretch of corridor and structural beams. "Why don't we skip the game and you can give me your mark and the women, too?"

"And deprive you of learning from my gambling skills?" Simon kept rolling with the cover, pushing his luck for as long as he could until—

He spotted Dorian.

Mouth taped, hands bound, guarded by a guy with an automatic weapon, she sat behind one of the structural beams beside another woman Konstantinou had taken.

Her eyes were wide and white in the dark, and they communicated a fierce indignation and fighting spirit that told him everything he needed to know. She was ready to take on these guys. No holds barred.

He just needed to give her an opening.

A damn fine time to discover he could read this incredible woman's mind.

Ah, hell. Simon squeezed the trigger on the weapon he'd hidden by his hip, taking the gunman down with a surprise shot to the leg before he spun to take out Tex. Dorian's friend shrieked behind her gag while Dorian sprang to her feet, her hands already half undone as she went for her gun under her dress.

Simon turned on his heel to face Konstanti-nou's guys. Even through the gunfire he could hear Dorian shouting a cry for help into her cell phone. She must have freed her gag to call for backup.

The whole shoot-out probably took less than a minute, but the movements seemed to go by in slow motion. Gunfire lit up the basement with occasional bursts of light, illuminating the action in a strange, strobelike reality. Simon felt a bullet wing his shoulder as he ducked and rolled to take out the two guards with Konstantinou. Women screamed behind him, and he nearly pissed himself to hear the fire of an automatic weapon, the shots pinging with echoing intensity in the basement.

Heart burning with more fear for Dorian than pain from the bullet he'd taken, Simon took out Konstantinou with a kick to the groin. A cheap as hell shot that a man could get away with using when the odds were this far out of his favor.

Simon ripped a gun out of one of the fallen guard's hands to crack across the back of Konstantinou's skull. The bastard would stand trial for what he'd done so no way would Simon let him take the easy way out by dying.

"Simon!" Dorian's shout broke through the

smoke and acrid burn of gunpowder, the sudden silence deafening.

His gut twisted at the fear in her voice, but at least that meant she was alive. He glanced around to find her holding an AK-47 over two other guards being wrapped in duct tape by her friend. In the distance he heard the thunder of footsteps clamoring down the stairwell and a second later their backup swarmed the place.

About time.

"Told you we'd nail the bastards," he shouted back, grinning because they were both alive and because he loved his job. Or maybe he was grinning because he was crazy about her.

"They hit you." She was standing over him all of a sudden, and he reached out to touch her since she looked a little shaky from the stress. Then, spotting his blood on her skirt where she knelt beside him, he realized she was holding him steady because he was dizzy as hell from blood loss.

"Great," he muttered, liking the feel of her cool hand on his forehead as she bent over him in her skintight sequin dress with a rip in one shoulder. "No telling what a guy will say when he's wounded. Doesn't blood loss act like truth serum or something?"

Dorian tore off a piece of his shirt, her hands probably working quickly, though everything felt slow to him.

"I sincerely hope so." She wound bandages around his shoulder while patrol officers and other detectives began searching the basement for any other suspects and cordoning off the crime scene. "Because I'd like to know—for real—if you're ever going to change your ways as a wild man. I've never seen a man take so many chances in the space of sixty seconds. Were you insane to start shooting before I even got myself all the way untied?"

Her jaw might be tight with anger, but there were also tears in her eyes.

"Too many questions in there. Yes, I'm insane. No, I can't change. But I swear I'd try to if I could for a woman as kick-ass as you."

Her watery smile damn near turned his heart over.

"I don't want you to change." She kept up pressure on his shoulder even though her bandage was doing a hell of a job on its own. "I thought you were brilliant just now even if you scared a decade off my life. In fact, I think for my next undercover assignment I'm going to take a page out of your book and play things a bit looser."

He groaned.

"I don't recommend my approach, Dor. And I have to say that if it was you sitting here bleeding right now—even with just a flesh wound—I'd be freaking out."

"That's the blessing of being a grounded type," she admitted, her cleavage truly spectacular as she leaned over to kiss his cheek. His mouth. And yeah, her jaw quivered even if the stubborn woman wouldn't admit to any weakness. "I'm too practical to get worked up over a little scratch—and I'm intrigued about blood loss acting as truth serum."

His head tipped back against one of the structural supports, and Dorian waved one of her cop friends over to secure Konstantinou. He suspected she was keeping everyone else at bay with her badge and a scowl he knew all too well. For once, her stand-back glare wasn't directed at him. It was a feeling he could get used to.

"Yeah? You have more burning questions for me?" Her scent was so sweet he wanted to pull her against him and lay with her for twenty-four hours straight. He wrapped a curl around his finger, not caring if her cop friends saw him staring at Dorian like she was the only woman in the world.

Of course, she *was* as far as he was concerned.

"I sure do. Do you think if I take you home with

me next time you'll run out on me again?" She traced his lips with her fingertip then smoothed a path down his neck.

"If I was that lucky a second time, I wouldn't walk back out your door in a million years, babe."

She blinked fast, her eyes so pretty and glistening.

"Really? What if you were undercover?"

"That's a tough one. But I think I might have to drag you into my cover with me so I could keep you by my side. You could be my drug dealer or the woman I was having an affair with—"

"Or the local dominatrix…just to make sure I don't always have the position of weakness."

"Whatever floats your boat, gorgeous." He saw her waving over the EMTs and realized he wasn't nearly finished with everything he had to say. "Wait. Dor?"

"Yeah?"

"I wouldn't want you to lose even a drop of blood for my sake, but the truth serum effect…well, it would be cool if I could ask you anything sometime, too." Was that too much to ask? Not that he thought she would lie to him other times. But they'd avoided the issues between them…the attraction…for so long they'd gotten skilled at weaving away from the whole subject.

"I'm game. Consider it my present to you for saving my butt on this mission."

"If I take you home with me when I get sprung from the ER, would you stay?" The question shook him out of his blood-loss torpor enough to make him realize he was nervous for the answer. He'd been chasing Dorian for so long, screwing up and then trying to regain lost ground, that he knew he'd probably used up all his chances. If she didn't want him now, he'd regret it for the rest of his life.

And then he'd just keep chasing her.

"How about if I go to the ER with you and hang around to drive you home, then you can find out the answer for yourself?" Her fingers walking up his chest felt damn good.

He smiled.

"Yes, ma'am. I like that idea." He pulled her down to him to kiss her mouth, effectively blocking his view of the EMT guys vying to get their hands on him.

Damn it.

When Dorian backed away, she whispered, "No more true confessions, though, until it's just you and me, okay?"

"Okay." He loved that private side of her, the one that made sure she kept her wild moments just for him. Still, he couldn't suppress his own impulse to tease her. "Did I tell you I bet everything I had on you on a poker round with Konstantinou, by the way?"

He held out his arm for the EMT guys to take his vitals, but he kept his gaze trained on every sexy inch of Dorian in form-fitting sequins. She scowled down at him as she stood but her eyes didn't contain all that much heat to go with her glare. He couldn't wait to get her alone.

"You bet on me?"

"Double or nothing. I had to have you for myself." He winked at her and waved away the oxygen the EMT guys wanted to shove in his mouth. "And that's no lie."

EPILOGUE

"So what else did I say while I was bleeding like a stuck pig?"

Dorian couldn't ward off a grin as they pulled into the palm tree–lined parking area of the downtown precinct of the LVMPD. She'd made a game of taunting Simon with alleged sensual promises he'd made while loopy from blood loss. She knew being injured on the job had pissed him off by taking a small chink out of his seemingly impenetrable pride, but the game had cheered him when she assured him he promised her multiple orgasms before they fell into bed for the night and even more the next day.

He'd made good on his fictional promise after the hospital had cleared him, and she was looking forward to seeing how he could possibly top last night.

Of course, first she had to file her paperwork at the precinct. She'd had help to make the arrests last night when she needed to get to the hospital with Simon, but someone had called her to let her know one of the hotel staffers who'd provided Konstantinou with a key to the basement level had also admitted to spiking Dorian's drink. Apparently the server had been on the payroll for months, occasionally spiking drinks or otherwise stalling attractive women he thought might be open to the idea of extra "work."

This afternoon she needed to tie up the rest of the details on the case and congratulate whichever one of her friends had won their bet for the week off. As much as Dorian would have enjoyed seven days of freedom to see how many more sensual favors she could receive and give back, too, she couldn't have left Simon last night after he'd saved her. Her life. Her case. And quite possibly her heart.

"Hmm. You rambled so much I hardly know where to begin," she teased. "But there was a lot about how much your shoulder hurt."

His eyebrows knit together as he put the car in Park.

"Real men don't feel pain. Now I know you're making stuff up." There was a pale cast to his tan despite his words, his coloring attesting to how close he'd come to death. His strength had saved him when other men might still be laid low.

"Really?" She fluttered her eyelashes for innocent effect. "Because you told me you'd need to rest your shoulder to recover and that I might need to explore some…um…oral options in the pleasure department while you got better."

"Yeah?" He massaged his upper arm where a bandage lurked beneath his T-shirt. "On second thought, it does ache every now and again."

She leaned across the console to kiss him, her heart already skipping wildly in her chest. The inside of the air-conditioned car heated up as much as the blazing temps of a Vegas summer outside.

"I don't know how I'm going to wait eight hours," she confided, seriously loving the fact that she could play games with Simon. Her world had been so intense for so long that it seemed freeing to laugh and joke and play.

And the sex…

She'd be having hot flashes all day at this rate.

"If it's any consolation, I guarantee this day's going to be even longer for me since you planted that particular sexual image in my head."

Breaking away, she stared into his eyes, liking everything about him. Why hadn't she seen past his easygoing facade to the committed, honorable guy beneath? She'd fallen for him even before the time she'd picked him up in a dive bar, but she'd let her pride get in her way to see that she wasn't the only one working through some big problems that night.

Maybe they'd both just needed time to come to terms with the inevitable. They were diametric opposites in so many ways but that didn't stop a core respect, caring and flat-out lust for each other. Who said a couple needed to share all the same qualities to create a strong relationship? For Dorian's part, she was ready to try.

"I'll make it worth your while," she vowed, silently promising herself to see beyond people's outward attitudes to the deeper core that mattered.

She'd missed that lesson with her mother and she could only hope that somehow her mom knew Dorian would grow to be a more understanding person one day. Testing out a real relationship with Simon made her think she'd already become that better person. But for good measure, she was keeping in touch with Evangeline to help show her she had friends and options for her future that didn't involve selling her body. That felt like the right way to come to peace with her mother, too.

Plus, Simon would make sure the Bureau followed through on their end to help recover the lost prostitutes who'd gone missing this year. Konstantinou would give up their whereabouts when he was interrogated. She would make sure of that. As much as Dorian was thrilled to have captured the guys behind the awful scheme, her heart still hurt for those other women who hadn't had the benefit of police protection, and she wouldn't rest until they received help to come back home.

"Looks like we've got company." Simon pointed out the back window to a Ford Explorer pulling up behind them and then leaned in for one more quick kiss. "You'd better get cracking at those eight hours because I'm not waiting an extra second when I come pick you up."

"You're on, Ramsey." Sliding out of the car, Dorian hopped onto the curb in front of the stone-and-stucco facade and waved to Kim Wong who seemed to be arriving with…a man?

Sure enough, Kim sat in the passenger seat of her SUV, a purple baseball cap on her head, while Captain Marc Cardenas, the man assigned to pose as Kim's boyfriend/bodyguard on her case, chauffeured her to work. The pair kissed so deeply Dorian felt like a voyeur and turned her eyes back to the parking lot in time to see Simon accelerate onto 9th street at the same time a sporty red BMW convertible drove into the station's parking lot.

"Hey, Dorian," Kim called, jumping down to the pavement from the SUV's high running board before her brawny companion peeled away. "I see the love bug bit your butt this weekend, too?"

Kim spun the brim of her cap to the back so that the word *Angel* disappeared behind her head and the word *Naughty* took its place.

Dorian could only shake her head.

"Amazingly, it looks like we weren't the only victims of lust on the job." Dorian nodded toward the red BMW headed their way a little too fast for parking lot safety.

The driver took full advantage of the German engineering, however, sliding the car into place mere inches from the curb. With the convertible top down, Kim and Dorian had an excellent view of the muscular legs on the star cyclist athlete that Clarissa Rivers had been pretending to be married to during her undercover assignment.

From the borderline make-out that ensued, apparently Clarissa had changed her mind about male athletes. She grinned like a woman in love as she said a starry-eyed goodbye to her new Romeo and practically floated out of the car.

"Don't tell me." Kim shook her head in disbelief. "How long have we been working together and complaining over the total lack of romance in a lady cop's life?"

"What?" Clarissa shook off the morning-after

glow with considerable effort. "Did I miss something?"

Kim and Dorian laughed as they all headed toward the station.

"Only some bizarre proof that good things happen in threes. Kim and I both rolled into work with male companionship, and neither of us can remember when something like that has happened for one of us, let alone all three."

"Must be cover assignments agree with us?" Clarissa suggested, running her fingers through her hair as they entered the station through the central glass doors.

"Either that or hell froze over," Kim quipped, heading for her desk in an interior that seemed dim compared to the blistering sun outdoors. "So who won the bet while I was, uh…out of commission last night?"

Dorian and Clarissa exchanged a look just as Captain Pearson charged out of his office like a bull on steroids. The hat pulled down tightly over his head didn't hide the blue vein throbbing in his right temple. His phone rang incessantly from the office behind him as he entered the mass of mostly empty desks where the majority of the detectives did their paperwork.

"Anyone ever heard of paperwork? I had a

boatload of patrol cars screaming all over town this weekend and not one of you could be bothered with filing reports?"

Dorian knew her hospital alibi was rock solid, but before she could offer it up, both Kim and Clarissa leaped to their own defenses, spilling snippets of fights and arrests and shooting that Dorian couldn't wait to hear in full detail.

The *other* more personal details were bound to be interesting, as well.

"Wait a minute." Dorian entered the fray, determined to be reasonable and prevent the whole precinct from overhearing even if there were only a handful of cops milling around the station today. "It sounds like none of us has won the bet yet, right?" A great idea was brewing in her head and she was certain her love-struck friends were going to unanimously approve it.

"Not me," Kim and Clarissa answered together in perfect synch as they dodged a cop coming through with a local boozehound who appeared to need some sobering up.

Around them the station seemed to go a shade quieter as if ears strained all over the precinct to hear what was going on. A coffeepot gurgled in the distance while the captain's phone kept ringing.

"Then the week off could go to whoever types

the fastest since we all closed our cases." Knowing her own speed at the keyboard was formidable, Dorian couldn't deny she was tempted. "But I think we all know who is most deserving of that week off."

Clarissa smiled while Kim filled in the blank.

"The cranky cop the love bug failed to bite this weekend." She nodded in agreement, her ponytail bobbing beneath her purple baseball hat.

Clarissa made her way toward the captain, her pink cheeks flushed with good health and happiness now that her hives were gone.

"Captain, we'd like to give *you* the vacation week since you've been working your tail off to orchestrate the big sting. We'll cover for you while you…you know…remind your wife you still know how to be spontaneous and have fun."

The captain looked so serious for a moment Dorian worried he might take issue with the suggestion there was anything wrong in his personal life. Cops could be touchy, and Dorian really identified with the need to present a controlled front to the world.

She stepped closer to the captain, knowing how much he deserved time to save his marriage and remember why relationships were worth fighting for.

"In fact, I'm going to throw in a call to the florist and send some orchids over to your wife on your behalf. Wouldn't that be a nice way to let her know to expect a surprise coming her way?" She remembered Mrs. Pearson admiring the orchids at a police fund-raiser event a year ago.

"And I'm going to make you some dinner reservations at that new Italian place on Las Vegas Boulevard South." Kim shoved aside a sequined tennis visor on her desk and reached for the phone book.

The captain's stony features didn't soften, but the vein in his temple had quit throbbing. An expression of pure determination came over his face just before Clarissa ran to her cubicle.

"Act now and you'll also get a primo piece of tasteful lingerie to arrive while she's dressing for dinner." Clarissa pulled her cell phone from her purse. "Mrs. Pearson likes blue, right?"

The captain looked at each of them with the slow deliberation that made him such a great leader. The man never acted on impulse, but only with careful consideration.

"And you'll each get those reports filed?"

"I'm on it," Dorian assured him, ready to pull out all the stops to get him out the door. Her own wonderful weekend had her seeing the world through rose-colored glasses today, and she couldn't wait to share that happiness with everyone else. "You know my work ethic speaks for itself, Captain. Last night was an aberration."

"You should enjoy the good PR for the department after all the arrests this weekend," Kim added, hanging up the desk phone and hooking arms with Marc Cardenas, who'd followed her inside after parking her vehicle. "You'll be a hero in all the papers by tomorrow. Your dinner reservations are for seven o'clock, by the way."

Slowly, Captain Pearson took off his hat and hung it on the coatrack by his office door. His brown eyes glittered with new purpose.

"Very well then, ladies. I accept your offer." He strode toward the door with determined steps. "I've earned a few days off." He turned back to look at them before leaving, the hint of a smile finally curling one side of his mouth. "How much you want to bet my wife is going to like this idea?"

Clarissa let out a long wolf whistle while Kim took up a pep rally cheer along with the new man in her life. Heads popped up all around the station to see what the fuss was about, but Captain Pearson was already taking his cute butt out the door to fight for his happily ever after.

REQUEST YOUR FREE BOOKS!
2 FREE NOVELS PLUS 2
FREE GIFTS!

HARLEQUIN ROMANCE

From the Heart, For the Heart

YES! Please send me 2 FREE Harlequin Romance® novels and my 2 FREE gifts. After receiving them, if I don't wish to receive any more books, I can return the shipping statement marked "cancel." If I don't cancel, I will receive 4 brand-new novels every month and be billed just $3.57 per book in the U.S., or $4.05 per book in Canada, plus 25¢ shipping and handling per book and applicable taxes, if any*. That's a savings of over 15% off the cover price! I understand that accepting the 2 free books and gifts places me under no obligation to buy anything. I can always return a shipment and cancel at any time. Even if I never buy another book from Harlequin, the two free books and gifts are mine to keep forever.

114 HDN EEV7   314 HDN EEWK

Name	(PLEASE PRINT)	
Address		Apt.
City	State/Prov.	Zip/Postal Code

Signature (if under 18, a parent or guardian must sign)

Mail to the **Harlequin Reader Service®:**
IN U.S.A.: P.O. Box 1867, Buffalo, NY 14240-1867
IN CANADA: P.O. Box 609, Fort Erie, Ontario L2A 5X3

Not valid to current Harlequin Romance subscribers.

Want to try two free books from another line?
Call 1-800-873-8635 or visit www.morefreebooks.com.

* Terms and prices subject to change without notice. NY residents add applicable sales tax. Canadian residents will be charged applicable provincial taxes and GST. This offer is limited to one order per household. All orders subject to approval. Credit or debit balances in a customer's account(s) may be offset by any other outstanding balance owed by or to the customer. Please allow 4 to 6 weeks for delivery.

Your Privacy: Harlequin is committed to protecting your privacy. Our Privacy Policy is available online at www.eHarlequin.com or upon request from the Reader Service. From time to time we make our lists of customers available to reputable firms who may have a product or service of interest to you. If you would prefer we not share your name and address, please check here. ☐

HR07